CONTENTS

KEEPER TYREE   1

All Things Western   2

AND MORE   3

ALL RIGHTS RESERVED   5

Dedicated to: 7

Chapter 1   8

Chapter 2   25

Chapter 3   42

Chapter 4   52

Chapter 5   59

Chapter 6   90

Chapter 7   102

Chapter 8   111

Chapter 9   122

Chapter 10   140

Chapter 11   158

Chapter 12   174

Chapter 13	183
Chapter 14	196
Chapter 15	203
Chapter 16	231
Chapter 17	236
Author's Note	241

KEEPER TYREE

ALL THINGS WESTERN

By S. Cox

ThunderTree
Reuben Hayes
Sheriff Tyree

By Sandra Cox

Western Romance

Gwen Slade, Bounty Hunter
TumbleStar
Silverhills
Return to Silverhills

Time Travel Western Romance

Montana Shootists
Sundial
Geller's Find

Shapeshifter Modern Day Western Romance

Mateo's Law
Mateo's Blood Brother
Mateo's Woman

AND MORE

Romantic Suspense with a touch of Paranormal
The Crystal
Paranormal Romance
Tall, Dark and Undead

Romantic Suspense
Queen of Diamonds

Young Adult Series
Cats of Catarau
Shardai
Akasha
Makita

Young Adult
Minder

Anthologies
Parallels: Felix Was Here

Nonfiction
Flower Gardens and More

Retired
Odin Cats

Sunset
Vampire Island
Moon Watchers
Vampire Bay
Power Stones
Boji Stones
Rose Quartz
Black Opal
Mutants
Love, Lattes, and Mutants
Love, Lattes, and Danger
Love, Lattes, and Angel
Ghost For Sale

ALL RIGHTS RESERVED

Acknowledgement and thanks to:

Beta Readers
Dawn Beca
Shane Blanchard
D. L. Finn
Elizabeth Seckman
Chris Yockey

Proofer
Chris Yockey

Research Assistant
Shane Blanchard

IT Guru
Sonya Blanchard

DEDICATED TO:

J.Q. Rose, author, friend and honorary cousin

CHAPTER 1

Dodge City, March 1880

No tinny piano. No rotgut whiskey. No barroom brawls. Just peace, quiet and the early morning sun, shining through white ruffled curtains, warming the back of Keeper Tyree's neck and soothing his arthritis. He brought his coffee to his lips and sighed with pleasure. Like his landlady it was strong and full-bodied, just the way he liked.

Molly, the owner of the boarding house he resided in, came by with the coffeepot. She winked at him and, giggling, moved out of reach when he went to pat her fanny, disappearing into the kitchen where the smells of breakfast potatoes, steak and eggs loosened his muscles and had his stomach growling in anticipation.

Heels clicked on the spotless, honey-colored wood floor. A woman so thin, she'd be lost if she turned sideways, approached from the doorway. She'd be striking if slashes of grief didn't line her mouth and despair turn her eyes to a wintry slate blue. Still, they met his, direct and unswerving. A black ribbon held back hair as dark as a raven's wing, except for streaks of white at the temples. Cheekbones sharp enough to cut paper held no color.

She stopped in front of him.

"Ma'am." The chair scraped across the floor as he pushed to his feet.

"Are you Keeper Tyree?"

"I am."

"Do you know of Josiah Pardee?"

"I do." He stuck his hands in his pockets and rocked on his heels, his voice rough and raspy from too much whiskey and too many cigars.

"He killed my son over a saloon tart. My boy wasn't even armed." The woman looked brittle as dry timber. He fancied if he rested a hand on her arm it would break like kindling. Only her voice and eyes showed emotion. A fire burning almost out of control leaped bright and violent behind her eyes, taking them from wintry blue-gray to heated sapphire.

"You have my sympathy."

The almond-shaped eyes drilled into him. "I don't want your sympathy. I want your gun. I want that man as cold and dead as my son."

Women. Warm as a soft summer night unless a loved one was threatened then vengeful as a puma whose kit has been harmed.

"Why don't you sit down and tell me exactly what you are after." He motioned toward the chair on the other side of the table.

"I just told you. I want him dead." She pulled out the chair and dropped into it.

He did the same.

"Molly," he bellowed. "Another cup of coffee."

With a swish of skirts, Molly came bustling out. The wooden-handled tin-iron coffeepot in one hand, a white ceramic mug as sturdy as Molly herself in the other. She plunked the cup down and poured with the expertise of long practice. "Can I get you something to eat, dearie?"

"No thank you." The woman gave Molly a tight smile.

"You sure? If a good wind came along, it could knock you over."

She shook her head, the tight smile still in place.

Molly brushed at a nonexistent crumb on the table then turned to Tyree. "You ready for yours?"

"In a few minutes."

She nodded and zitted to a table on his right where another boarder had just sat down. Molly was always in a hurry, even in bed.

"I'm told you are a gunslinger by trade."

"When I'm not bounty hunting, my gun is for hire." He fingered his coffee cup.

"Is it for hire now?"

"I have no problem going after Pardee."

"How much do you charge?"

"Five hundred plus expenses."

"How much will expenses run me?" She sat at the edge of her chair, her back ramrod straight.

"Right to the point. I like that."

"Well?" She didn't smile just waited for an answer.

"Not much. For the most part grub and bullets."

"I've got a hundred in the cookie jar."

Before she could say more, he interrupted, holding

up his hand. "Never tell a stranger where you keep your money, Mrs…"

"O'Donnell. Cathleen O'Donnell." She held her hand out across the table.

He grasped it. A small hand lost in his big paw. Not rough. But not as soft as it could be either. A working hand.

"You're right of course. You must think I'm emptyheaded. I'm not." Her shoulders straightened even more if that was possible and her chin notched up.

"No," he responded in his raspy voice, his expression unsmiling and straightforward. "Emptyheaded never entered my mind." Inconsolable. Grieving nearly to the point of madness but not emptyheaded. Keen intelligence shown from those wintry eyes that changed from gray to blue and back again depending on her emotions.

"I don't have five hundred."

"Well now." He tipped his chair back on two legs. "I don't work for less."

"I'll get it somehow." Determination coated her voice and those changing eyes grew darker. "I can give you a hundred and I'll raise the rest."

"And how do you propose to do that?"

She cleared her throat and looked him in the eye. "I'll do anything to avenge my son's death. Anything." Color flooded her face.

"Have you made this offer to anyone else?" His chair came down with a thump and his gruff voice came out gruffer than usual.

"No. I need someone that's fast with his gun, ruthless and won't be held back by principles. When I asked around, your name kept cropping up. I want you."

He rubbed his freshly shaved chin unsure whether to laugh or curse. "I have principles, but they're my own not those set up by pious bible thumpers, but as to the rest that's close enough."

Thrumming his fingers on the table, he studied her, 'til she squirmed uncomfortably. Finally, he said, "As far as your offer, it won't be necessary. Nor would I accept it."

If possible, her face flamed even brighter.

"There's a bounty on his head. Pay me the hundred. I'll collect the bounty and we'll call it even."

Relief flooded her features.

He snorted. Good thing he wasn't easily offended.

"Does your husband know you are here?" He wouldn't be much of a man if he knew what she was about.

"I'm a widow." She stood. "When can we start?"

He too pushed to his feet fighting back irritation. "There is no we. Tonight, I'll make the rounds of the saloons that he frequented, starting with the Long Branch. See if I can't get information on where he's at now. If I find out where he holes up, I'll head out at first light."

"Come to my place tomorrow morning and I'll pay you." With an impatient gesture, she pushed at a wisp of hair that had the temerity to come loose.

"Where's it located?"

"Two miles south of Dodge."

"I'll be there."

"Good day, Mr. Tyree."

"Good day, Mrs. O'Donnell."

A faint scent of lemon verbena, along with the brisk click of heels, grew fainter as she walked away. He shifted his weight, his hands on his hips. An intriguing woman Mrs. O'Donnell. Not in his line of country, of course. He liked women with meat on their bones. You'd have to shake the sheets to find her. His gaze lingered on the last glimpse of her before she disappeared through the dining room and into the lobby. Still and all she intrigued him. Intrigued might be too strong a word, more like discombobulated him. Like putting on an itchy suit and starched shirt and marching into church on Sunday. Yeah, that was it. Having settled that to his satisfaction he bellowed, "Molly, I'll take breakfast now."

~*~

He threw his legs over the bed, held his head and groaned. At forty-six he was too damn old to be drinking that much rotgut. Ten years older than the average life span in his profession. Still and all it had paid off. Pardee, drunk on his ass to hear one of the saloon girls tell it, indulged in a little pillow talk. Pillow talk, that with a little sweet talk and a couple double eagles, she'd been happy to share. Pardee had headed for the Kansas Badlands until things cooled down. Apparently, the townspeople didn't take kindly to a sixteen-year-old being gunned down, especially one that wasn't even wearing a gun. It had happened when Keeper had been out of town and the news had moved on to the next scandal by the time he'd got back.

He pulled up tan canvas pants over long johns, shoved his feet into worn boots and strode to the window. A gold ball of glory flirted on the pink-colored horizon visible between the timber joists of a building going up across the street. The quiet of morning in direct contrast to the shootings and rabble rousting of last night. He splashed water in the basin and washed up, finished getting dressed then headed downstairs, a flask in his vest pocket. A little hair of the dog in his coffee would offset the hammers pounding at his skull.

He pulled out the hard-backed chair at his favorite table in the dining room and dropped down. From here he could see both the entryway and the kitchen. Part of the reason he was an aging gunman instead of a resident of Boot Hill was an abundance of caution. Drink might slow him down but he could always function.

Molly saw him from the kitchen door, disappeared and whisked back with the coffeepot and poured him a cup, steam rising and carrying the aromatic fragrance of dark beans.

"Thanks, Molly."

"I missed you last night."

"I went out."

"I can tell. You wreak of rotgut. It's coming out of your pores." She wrinkled her nose.

"Well, I washed up and put on a clean shirt. Can't do anything about my pores." He took a gulp of strong, scalding liquid. "That's good coffee." Then added a healthy dollop from his flask.

"Want some breakfast?"

"I'd take a beefsteak —"

"Rare?"

"Yeah. Thanks."

"Put your clothes outside your door and I'll wash 'em."

"Again, thanks. You'll make someone a wonderful wife."

"But not you."

"I'm not looking for marriage. Is that a problem?" He sat down his cup. Molly was a widow. He'd been at the boarding house for over a year now. They'd always enjoyed a good romp, with no strings, for most of that time. It was a comfortable arrangement. It would be inconvenient to find a new place but not as inconvenient as having a woman hanging out for a ring.

She gave out a great guffaw that had her ample bosom shaking. "You should have seen your face." She walked away shaking her head and still laughing.

A few minutes later she returned with a beefsteak that nearly mooed at him.

"I'm going to be gone for a while," he told her as she plopped the plate in front of him, the steak still sizzling.

"You going after Pardee?"

"You're smart as well as beautiful. How'd you

figure that one out?"

A young couple walked in and sat at a table near the door.

"Be right with ya," Molly called out.

The man nodded and held up his hand.

"Cathleen O'Donnell comes in my place for the first time looking for you. Pardee killed her son. I can put two and two together and get four. You be careful, Keeper."

"I'm not worried about Pardee."

"I'm not talking about Pardee."

Before he could respond she pivoted and bustled away.

Now what was that supposed to mean? Keeper shook his head. There was just no figuring women. He wolfed down his steak, gathered his things and rode the two miles out of town to the O'Donnell place. Topping a low rise, he reined in and looked down.

Below stood a rundown cabin, barn and stable. A homestead too small to be considered a farm. Scrawny chickens pecked at pebbles and a pig wandered around, its kinked tail wiggling. A medium-sized black dog sat on the porch.

He nudged his horse with his heels. The bay tossed his head then loped down the incline. As he approached the house, the dog barked, a loud bay of warning.

A stooped, gray-haired man stepped out, a rifle in the crook of his arm.

Keeper reined in at the front of the porch.

"Can I help you, mister?"

"I'm looking for Mrs. O'Donnell."

"And you would be?"

"Keeper Tyree. You?"

"Henry. Henry O'Donnell. I'm her father-in-law. We're having breakfast. Please get down and join us, Mr. Tyree."

"Well, I've already had breakfast but I wouldn't turn down a cup of coffee." He swung out of the saddle, tied his horse to the post and strode onto the porch, his heels clumping against rough wood.

Mr. O'Donnell held out a hand. Tyree shook it. The man's grasp firm. His hand callused. The hand of a man that worked the land. He'd take calluses any day. He didn't trust men whose hands were soft and well-tended.

"Mr. O'Donnell."

"Call me Henry."

"Henry."

"Won't you come in, Mr. Tyree?"

"Keeper or Tyree. There's no need for mister."

He followed Henry in. While the exterior resembled a worn-out old woman, the interior glowed with clean and polish. A speck of dust wouldn't dare raise its head. Sunbeams streamed through the east kitchen window onto a high-varnished pine table that held a pretty multicolored ceramic vase at its center. A cute little girl with pigtails as blue-black as her mother's sat with a plate full of eggs and bacon in front of her. She looked up. A milk mustache ringed the smile she gave him.

Keeper smiled back. He might be an old

curmudgeon, but he had a weakness for little girls. They were pure of heart, hadn't yet learned to use their wiles on unsuspecting males or grown bitter from being worn down by life.

"Hello," she said.

"Hello."

"Who are you?"

"Aislinn, that's rude," her mother reproved.

For the first time he glanced at Mrs. O'Donnell. Irritated unease ran through him. The men's trousers and shirt she wore fit her thin frame like a glove and looked much more appealing than they would have on a heavier-set lady. They disquieted him and made him aware of her as a woman. Something he didn't want to think about. His life in that compartment was taken care of. Then there was the fact that she was wearing them at all, like she planned on doing considerable time in the saddle. Maybe she wore them around the homestead when doing chores. He grabbed that thought and hung on.

"Coffee, Mr. Tyree?"

"Please."

"Why is it rude, Momma?" the little girl piped up.

Before Mrs. O'Donnell could respond, Keeper bent down and shook her hand. "My name is Keeper Tyree."

"That's an odd name."

"Aislinn!"

"So, I've been told." He gave her a wide grin. One he didn't let loose very often.

"Why were you named Keeper?" Her legs swinging, she kicked against the back of the chair.

"Aislinn Sue!"

"I guess my momma thought I was."

"Thought you were what?"

"A keeper."

She giggled at this then swiveled toward her mother. "Am I a keeper, Momma?"

"Of course, you are, my darling." The frozen features thawed, her lips turned up and an unexpected light lit her eyes making them glisten like sunlight on water. A quiver ran under his skin and arrowed to his belly. He frowned. He hadn't had that particular feeling since he was a younker of fifteen and had a crush on Amy Lou Harrington.

"Are you alright, Mr. Tyree?" Mrs. O'Donnell gave him a curious look.

"Yes, ma'am."

"Would you like some breakfast?" She handed him a large brown mug.

"Thank you, but I've already ate."

He took a gulp. Rich, hot brew rolled down his throat and settled into his belly. "That's good coffee."

"Thank you, Mr. Tyree."

"You are welcome, Mrs. O'Donnell."

"I'll grab your money and my things and be ready to go."

Dammit to hell, he knew this wasn't going to be easy. The woman was more stubborn than a mule. Irritation rose, tightening muscles and jangling nerves. "Just the money. I thought I made myself clear. I work alone. You aren't going."

"I thought I made myself clear. I am." She stood

hands on hip. Those magnificent eyes darkening and sparking.

"Looks like I made a trip out here for nothing." He sat the cup on the table and wheeled on his heel and headed for the door.

"Wait. I'll get your money." Her voice held resignation. She opened a pine cabinet door and pulled out a blue ceramic cookie jar.

"Mrs. O'Donnell, I believe I mentioned, you shouldn't tell a stranger where you keep your money. That goes for showing as well."

"He's got a point there, Cathleen." Henry filled his plate with bacon, eggs and a slice of bread before sliding into a chair next to his granddaughter.

"Are you saying I can't trust you?" Ignoring her father-in-law's comment, she pulled out a circle of bills.

He rocked on his heels and forced himself not to curse as he longed to.

"Of course, you can trust me, but you don't know that."

"I'm a good judge of character, Mr. Tyree."

"Says every woman ever born," he muttered.

Henry turned a chuckle into a cough.

"If I didn't trust you, you wouldn't be here."

"I thought I was ruthless and not held back by principles."

"Cathleen." Henry's voice held shock.

"That doesn't mean you aren't painfully honest."

His lips quirked. He liked that description. It was pretty much true.

"Why are you giving Mr. Keeper our cookie jar money?" Aislinn reached for her toast and crunched down.

"He's doing a job for me."

"What job?"

"He's hunting someone."

"You hunt people, Mr. Tyree?"

"I'm a bounty hunter, little missy." It sounded better than gunslinger and it happened to be true.

"What's a bounty hunter?"

"You ever seen a wanted poster?"

"Yes, they have pictures of bad men."

"That's what a bounty hunter does. He goes after the bad men."

She thought about this for a moment, her little brow wrinkled then finally asked, "Do they have female bounty hunters?"

"Well now," he rubbed his chin, his whiskers making a rasping noise. "I only know one. Gwen Slade, but she's a dam—darn good one. In fact, she lived around these parts till recently." He had a lot of respect for her. She was steady, with nerves of steel and a foreshortened rifle named Betsy that she could twirl as fast as he could a six-gun.

"That's what I'm going to be when I grow up." She gave a decisive nod then went back to her breakfast.

Mrs. O'Donnell frowned at him.

He threw his hands in the air. There was no winning this one. He took the smart way out and kept his mouth shut.

She handed him the money. "Good luck."

He nodded and stuck the money in his vest pocket. "Well, I'd best be on my way."

"Where is he?" Cathleen stuck the cookie jar back into the cabinet.

He gave her a long look. "I don't think that's information I'm willing to share with you. Good day."

"I'll walk you out." Henry pushed back his chair and headed for the door.

As he strode through it, Aislinn called, "Goodbye, Mr. Tyree."

"Goodbye, missy."

The men's heels clumped across the porch. Keeper trotted down the steps, gathered his horse's reins and swung into the saddle.

Henry placed a hand on the big bay's shoulder and said in a voice that wouldn't carry, "Don't be put off by Cathleen's brusque manner. Her husband, my son," his eyes grew sad and the skin around his mouth went slack before he straightened his shoulders, "died three years ago of influenza, liked to have killed her. They'd married when they were no more than kids. Both seventeen. Loved one another from the moment they set eyes on each other. And now the loss of the boy— I'm not rightly sure how she's survived it. Find Pardee. Hopefully it will give her closure."

"I intend to."

Mrs. O'Donnell stood in the doorway, her hand on her daughter's shoulder. He pulled on the brim of his hat. "Ma'am."

She nodded. The little girl waved. He tipped his hat to her too then tapped his horse with his heels and galloped away, heading north.

He rode till midday then stopped at a stream so clear he saw a turtle swimming along the bottom. While his horse drank, he filled his canteen, wet his bandana and wiped his face. "Damn." The cold water made him blink and toss off any lethargy from the whiskey. Flat landscape allowed him to see a flock of birds fluttering into the sky behind him as if they'd been startled.

He put his hand over his eyes to shield them from the sun and squinted at the bright globe of light. It was unlikely anyone was following him, but not impossible. Leading his horse around a bend in the creek, he waited. Being cautious kept him alive.

He pulled out a worn gold watch. Twelve-ten. He waited till it said twelve-twenty. No one had come into view. Time to move. He got on his horse and headed on. If he made twenty miles a day, he'd be in the badlands in five days.

Through the afternoon, he kept looking over his shoulder. Someone was back there. He'd bet his shirt on it. Not that he'd seen any signs since the birds had flown up as if disturbed. Just a gut feeling. And he'd learned never to ignore his gut. He'd ignored it once, years ago, and still had the scar from an arrow in his shoulder to prove it. He bided his time and looked for a likely place to make camp.

As sunset approached, he found it. A couple of trees and a boulder. Perfect for his needs.

With a suddenness that always surprised, the sun disappeared leaving a line of crimson on the horizon before everything turned inky black. One by one stars popped with brilliant intensity.

He saw to his horse, built a fire and made coffee from his dented old pot with its burned wooden handle. He poured himself a cup, threw his saddle on the ground, spread out a blanket, then disappeared into the dark and waited.

CHAPTER 2

Sipping strong, black coffee, he settled in. A twig snapped. He grabbed his gun and stood up. His horse snorted and the snapping came again as the stallion stepped on another small limb.

"Damn horse," he muttered under his breath and slunk back into the shadows.

This time he heard the thump of approaching horse's hooves. They grew louder as they came closer, stopping in the shadow. A few moments later a slender rider with a black duster and hat pulled low on his forehead walked around the campfire. He stopped, his back to Keeper. Keeper leaped, knocking the rider to the ground, face eating dirt.

"Who are you, mister, and why are you following me?" He put his boot on the stranger's back and pressed down.

"Can't breathe."

The voice, low and husky, held a familiar quality.

"Mrs. O'Donnell?" His eyebrows shot up toward his hairline.

He pulled her up, cursed long and fluently, finishing with, "What the hell are you doing here?"

Air whished out of her lungs and she took a couple

of deep breaths. "I told you, I want to end Pardee, the way he did my son."

He took a couple of deep breaths himself to keep from throwing down his hat and stomping on it, then clutching his hair and howling. After a minute, he got himself under control. "Have you ever killed a man, Mrs. O'Donnell?"

"No. But I won't have a problem killing Pardee."

Anguish, carried on the chill night breeze, washed off her in waves, till it hit his pores and filled him. "Ma'am, it stains your soul. You may think you want to do this, but it's not something you'd wish to live with."

As if to emphasize his words, a coyote howled in the distance. A lonely sound that emptied a body out and left one hollow and alone.

She shivered, then tossed her chin up. "What's your soul like?"

"Black as sin, ma'am. But I can live with it."

"I can too."

He shoved the gun he'd sheathed deep into the leather holster. He wore two Smith and Wesson five-inchers that gave him an edge when a fast draw was of the essence. A little handier with his right hand, he could use either proficiently and had on more than one occasion.

"I don't want you on my conscience."

Surprise flickered across her features. "You have no reason to have me on your conscience." She put her hands on her hips and studied him. "I'm told you're ruthless. So far I've seen nothing to back it up."

"Don't think for a moment I'm not. I've done

things you would never dream of." His voice roughened.

"I think the stories about you are exaggerated."

The humor of the situation hit him. No one had ever accused him of being soft. No one would dare. Molly'd had a point when she told him to watch out for Mrs. O'Donnell. The woman showed all the signs of being trouble.

"Far be it for me to disagree with a lady." He made a gallant motion toward the log with his hand. "Won't you sit down? I'll be happy to share my coffee with you."

"Let me get my cup. I brought some jerky, biscuits and peaches. Would you like some?"

"A meal fit for a king. I'd love some."

She paused on her way to her horse, the firelight outlining her form and leaving her face in shadows. "So, we're good?"

"Tomorrow you're going back."

~*~

The sun broke on the horizon, bright, big, and gold, like a wide smile. He'd swear mother nature was laughing at him.

He shook his head, wondering where things had gone wrong, when he'd lost control. Instead of heading back to her homestead—as she'd been told —Mrs. O'Donnell rode by his side, sitting easy in the saddle, her canvas duster open in the front and hanging over her legs, her black hat pulled low on her forehead. For once, she didn't look tense as a clock wound too tight. Probably cause she'd got her way.

Goldang, what a stubborn female. He'd never bumped up against one who had so little give in her cinch. She'd neatly boxed him in a corner. To go back now, he'd have to escort her home and then it would have been kicking and screaming over a saddle and he had no heart for it. Exasperation tightened the muscles between his shoulder blades and moved up his neck where arthritis added an uncomfortable twinge as he rode.

He pushed on, setting a hard pace, hoping she'd cry quits.

She didn't.

Still grumbling to himself hours later, they climbed a rise in the endless flatlands, the sun in the west barely warming the plains. The wheezing and heehawing of mules carried on the chill air followed by a high-pitched croaky, familiar voice. "Gee up, you lop-eared, four-hooved horrors." A whip snapped in the air.

Reining in, Keeper stared, rubbed his eyes and stared some more. Little surprised him in this cold, old world. But the sight of four women, three with their skirts hiked up, their shoulders against the back of a covered-wagon, pushing it up a creek bank, had shock jolting through his overburdened system.

He leaned forward in his saddle, cupped his hand and bellowed, "Maybell, what in blazes are you doing out here in the middle of nowhere?"

The brassy, well-endowed, middle-aged woman driving the wagon stopped yelling abuses at the mules, cupped her palm over her eyes to protect against bright sun and hollered right back, "Keeper? Keeper Tyree?"

"Heeya." He hit his horse on the flank with his hat and galloped down the hill.

Maybell jumped out of the wagon. Without a firm hand on the reins, the wagon rolled backwards. The women behind it dove to safety on the muddy banks.

With a grunt, he swung off his horse and Maybell sprang into his arms as Mrs. O'Donnell came trotting up.

"What are you doing out here, Keeper?"

"I believe that's what I was asking you."

"The girls and I are coming from Garden City. Decided to try our luck in El Dorado."

"On your own without any guards or protection?" He gave her a squeeze then set her aside.

"We had ole Moses, but he up and died on us. Got his rifle." She pointed at the seat where it lay.

"Ole Moses. He was with you a long time." He shook his head.

"Yes, he was. A good man. We buried him a day ago."

By now the girls had gathered round.

Mrs. O'Donnell reined in beside him.

Introductions were made. To his surprise, her face held no condemnation, even though Maybell's calling was abundantly clear. There was no makeup on her round face but it, like his own, was marked with hard-living and her eyes held a lifetime of knowledge.

"These are my girls." She gestured toward the

women with mud on their faces and clothes.

"Ladies." He swept off his hat and made an elaborate bow.

"Keeper, you remember Dora?"

The face with brown eyes and a knowing smile looked vaguely familiar.

Before he could respond, she sashayed up to him. "I remember you, handsome. Though, you might have been too drunk at the time to remember me."

Mrs. O'Donnell rolled her eyes. A wave of embarrassed heat rolled through his system. He cleared his throat. "Ladies, meet Mrs. O'Donnell."

"Mrs. O'Donnell." He motioned toward the other women, "Dora." He raised an eyebrow at the other two.

Maybell finished the introductions. "Betty Lou." She pointed at a woman with light brown hair of medium height and build. Or so she appeared under all the mud. "And, Juanita." She pointed at a young redhead, with a freckled face, clearly in her teens.

Mrs. O'Donnell made a sound of protest, an expression of distress on her pale features.

"Now, don't you worry, honey," Maybell reassured her. "Juanita here is our cook. As for the other gals," she shrugged well-rounded shoulders. "It's hard for a woman alone to make a living. If they were ever to choose an easier, but less lucrative trade, I'd back 'em. Course I'd expect a cut if they were waitressing a café I owned." Hands on hips, she winked.

Like the sun coming over a rise, Mrs. O'Donnell's features lightened. He knew she filled out her trousers in a most appealing way, but for the first time, it dawned on him, if she weren't as skinny as a scarecrow, she'd be a handsome woman and even thin her features were, well, striking.

He stomped his feet, shook off his unexpected thoughts then frowned in exasperation as the spindled, big back wheels settled with a squelch into the mud. "Let's see what we can do about that wagon. Maybell, hie back on that seat and I'll push you out."

Mrs. O'Donnell slipped out of the saddle.

"And what are you about?" he asked, hands fisted on hips.

"I'll pull the mules."

"Good idea." He nodded his approval.

Mrs. O'Donnell went to the front. With a rustle of skirts Maybell climbed into the wagon. The girls trudged through the sludge to the back.

He put his shoulder to the wagon, a girl on either side and Juanita at one of the back wheels. "Okay, Maybell, let's move it."

The whip cracked. "Let's go, you worthless things."

Mrs. O'Donnell's voice, as soothing as sunshine and soft as velvet, came in direct contrast. "Come on, my beauties, let's show them what you are capable of." For a moment he forgot to push, just listened to the unexpected sweetness of her voice, then a board quivered beneath his shoulder and he brought his mind back to the business at hand and threw his weight against the wagon.

The wheels made a sucking sound followed by a jolt of the wagon and the contrivance sloshed through the mud.

"Keep 'em moving. Keep 'em moving," he yelled.

The voices, one harsh and tinny, the other flowing like a brook, continued along with the heehawing of the mules. Then they were moving in good and earnest.

He grabbed Betty Lou as she nearly took another tumble in the mud.

"Thanks." Her voice breathless.

A groan of the wheels, a bump in the mud, a squish as the wheels popped and they were up the bank and on dry even ground.

The three women stood stoop-shouldered and panting, all of them wearing wide smiles.

Maybell jumped off the wagon, smiling just as wide, a gold front tooth showing.

"I see you still put your money where your mouth is." Keeper grinned at her.

"Among other spots." She winked and cocked a hip.

He shook his head. No telling where she kept the rest and truth be told, he didn't want to know.

"You girls need to get into some dry clothes." He followed Mrs. O'Donnell's gaze. The women were rubbing their wet arms, shivering.

The sun flirted with the horizon and the colors in the sky were strips of red, gold and glory.

"I'll build a fire." He flicked a ball of dirt off his fingers.

"We've got some beans, biscuits and applesauce. We'd be honored if you both would share vittles with us." Maybell made a vague sweeping gesture toward the wagon.

"That would be nice. Thank you." Mrs. O'Donnell gave a small smile.

He looked twice to make sure he'd seen her lips go up, but the smile came and went so quickly he couldn't rightly be sure. With the poker that seemed permanently attached to her spine, it surprised him she was taking the company of soiled doves with equanimity.

"Why don't you three go down the creek a ways and get cleaned up and I'll get supper together." Maybell directed.

"What can I do to help?" Mrs. O'Donnell stepped forward.

"If you wouldn't mind helping Keeper gather firewood, we can get those girls warmed up quick when they get back. That creek's going to be cold. Thanks, honey." Maybell turned and bustled into the wagon.

Mrs. O'Donnell looked at the one lone maple near the water's bank, a dubious expression on her face.

"We'll grab that handful of branches lying on the ground then throw some tumbleweeds on to get it going. There's plenty of them around." Keeper pointed at dry twigs interspersed with dead, rounded weeds that had no roots.

She nodded, walked briskly to the tree and began picking up small limbs.

By the time dark set in, they had a fire going. Its orange embers shooting up into the inky dark as if trying to connect with the glittering stars dotting the sky. Keeper stood close enough that the heat took the chill out of his bones. He listened to the pop and crackle, watched the colorful flames dance toward the heavens and knew contentment. There was just something about a campfire warding off the cold and the alone in the middle of a lonesome prairie that settled him.

The girls now back from cleaning up in the creek came out of the wagon laughing and chattering, wearing clean clothes, with blankets wrapped around them.

He swiped at a glob of dried mud on his sleeve. "Guess I'll go get cleaned up myself."

"Certainly, wouldn't hurt you none." Mrs. O'Donnell looked him up and down.

He shook his head and walked away. Woman had a tongue sharper than a rattlesnake's. He saw to the mules and horses then strode to the stream.

As he splashed water cold enough to make goose bumps stand up on his bare arms and torso, he wondered what she had been like before the loss of her boy. By the glimpse he'd gotten of her with her daughter, he'd say a warm, loving woman, even if she did come in a scrawny package. A little food could take care of that, he mused then jerked upright, the cold forgotten. What the hell was he thinking? Came from being around too many goldarn women.

He grabbed his saddlebag, threw on a clean shirt and strode back to camp. What he saw brought him up short. Maybell talking and the widow laughing. The fire glowing behind her, outlining her slender frame and pretty face. The tight lines around her mouth gone, her head thrown back, white teeth visible along with a long, lovely neck. He shifted uncomfortably. For the life of him, he couldn't figure out why she'd gotten under his skin so hard and fast. She was like an itch he couldn't scratch. It reminded him of a bad case of poison ivy he'd had as a younker.

He forgot his own itch and just watched her chat with Maybell. Who'd a thought a soiled dove and a strait-laced widow would have anything in common? He guessed there were times a woman just needed another woman.

Dora caught sight of him. "Keeper, grab your tin and come get something to eat."

He pulled a tin plate out of the saddlebag slung over his shoulder. "Got it right here."

While he'd been gone, they'd put on coffee and pulled out cans of applesauce, beans, some biscuits and jerky. Ms. O'Donnell had added her peaches.

"Looks good, ladies."

"I slaved over it all day." Maybell slapped her leg at her own joke.

The girls threw the blankets they'd wrapped around them on the ground and they all sat on them and ate. When they'd finished, Juanita brought out a battered guitar and began to play. In the background a coyote howled and the creek gently slapped against the shore.

Keeper shifted on the hard ground looking for a more comfortable spot.

Dora and Betty Lou disappeared into the wagon.

Silver gleamed in the moonlight as Maybell pulled out a flask. "Want a little in your coffee? Might soften the ground."

"Don't mind if I do." He held out his cup and she poured a dollop in it.

"Mrs. O'Donnell?" She held out the flask.

"I don't drink."

"I know you don't, honey, but sometimes it takes the edge off, dulls the pain." Her loud brash voice, gentle.

"How do you know I'm in pain?" Mrs. O'Donnell's whisper barely discernable above the strains of the guitar.

"Honey, it comes off you like hot thick air before a storm. Soaks right into my system. What's causing it if you don't mind my asking?"

"No. I don't mind. Ever heard of Josiah Pardee?"

"He's a bad one." Maybell shook her head.

"He killed my boy."

"Ahh. Well, if you are looking to even the score. Keeper's the man to do it."

"So, everyone keeps saying."

Keeper snorted at the doubt in her voice and Maybell laughed outright. Again, she held out the flask.

"Oh well, why not." Mrs. O'Donnell held out her cup.

Keeper looked at her in astonishment. She shrugged, took a sip and gasped, "It does warm the belly."

"It does indeed." Maybell let out a hearty laugh.

"What's your story. Why El Dorado?" Mrs. O'Donnell took another cautious sip.

"I'm buying me a mansion on the outskirts of town. I'm going to have a respectable establishment. Oh, I'll still be open for business, but the girls will be selective of the clientele. Also, gonna have a saloon in one room and a café in another. Juanita is going to run the café. I'll miss ole Moses. He worked as my bouncer and barkeep." For a moment her voice held sadness, then she straightened her shoulders and said more briskly, "But I'll find another. They won't replace ole Moses, but nobody could.

"Well, I'm going to turn in. It's been a long day, what with those long-eared critters getting stuck in the creek bed and all." She stood and stretched.

"Aren't you worried, traveling alone with just one rifle between you?" The firelight lit one side of her face as Mrs. O'Donnell gazed at Maybell.

"Nothing's certain in this world. I'm willing to run the risk and so is the girls." Maybell pointed her thumb in the direction of the wagon where the girls bedded down.

Mrs. O'Donnell stared into the fire for a long moment then straightened her shoulders. "We'll see you there."

Keeper nodded. "That's what I was thinking. Glad we're on the same page." He knew putting off the search for her son's killer must chafe her, but he also hadn't any doubt she'd do the right thing. She was that kind of woman.

"I appreciate that. Thankee kindly." Maybell's gold tooth glistened as she gave a grateful smile in the moonlight.

After sucking down everything on his plate, and taking a few gulps from his flask, he rolled out his bedroll and fell deep into sleep.

~*~

The smell of coffee and arthritis biting at his neck woke him. That and the stale scent of cheap perfume. His left side warm, his right side cold enough for frostbite. He rolled over and looked into Dora's flirty brown eyes then over her shoulder into Mrs. O'Donnell's censorious ones.

He jumped up like a jack-in-the-box toy. Though, he'd done nothing to feel guilty about. Hadn't done anything untoward the night before. Nor had he gotten boozy enough he'd forgotten about it. That's what came from being around a good woman. Always keeping a man off guard and feeling like a dunderhead when he'd done nothing to earn it.

Having properly settled the matter in his mind he yawned, stretched and pulled up his suspenders.

"Good morning, handsome." Dora sat up and put a hand on his thigh. He hopped back like a stuck toad and that made him mad all over again, acting like he was between hay and grass instead of a man full growed and then some.

"Dora, behave yourself." Maybell gave her a stern look, while pouring a mug of coffee that she held out to Keeper. When she spoke it was to Mrs. O'Donnell.

"Don't mind her, honey. Keeper isn't going to be doing anything he shouldn't while you're in camp."

"He's free to do as he likes." Her voice had an edge to it as cool as her breath that came out in a white cloud when she spoke.

Women. He threw his hands in the air. "I'll take that coffee when I get back, Maybell." He stomped into the underbrush, relieved himself then went to the stream and threw cold water on his face. The icy pellet-like drops threw every other discomfort right out the window.

Striding back into camp, he took the coffee Maybell had set on the pullout plank attached to the side of the wagon and took a gulp. Bent over a black kettle sitting over the fire, Maybell stirred industriously. She was a fine figure of a woman, he thought appreciatively as he took another swallow of strong, black coffee.

A shadow crossed his grave, raising goosebumps. He looked around surreptitiously. Once again, his eyes met artic blue. Dang the woman.

He raised his mug in her direction and she looked away.

"What are you fixing, Maybell darlin?"

"Oatmeal."

He bit back a sigh. At least, it would be hot. That in itself was a blessing on the trail.

"I'm sure it will be delicious."

"That sounded a little forced, Keeper. But that's all right. I know you're right partial to beefsteak." She laughed and he joined in.

The oatmeal was surprisingly tasty. Nice and sweet. She'd even added some peaches to it. He'd had a sweet tooth since he was a younker. Surprisingly, in spite of it, he had all his teeth. His hair might be thinning and his nose too big from being broken a time or two, but he took pride in his teeth. He had no intention of ending up with chompers or gumming his food.

A gust of wind whistled through the camp and down the back of his shirt. The sun showed no interest in breaking through an overcast, sullen sky. He rubbed his aching neck where the cold and damp jabbed at creaky joints and scarred bones. It was always worse in damp, chill weather. Ah well, better than being in Boot Hill and not having a care one way or another.

"Ladies, let's get a move on. Daylight's burning." He set the empty bowl and cup on the wagon plank.

In less time than he would have expected they were heading for El Dorado. Maybell drove the wagon with Dora and Juanita beside her and Betty Lou inside. Mrs. O'Donnell rode along the other side of the wagon.

"How long do you think it will take us to reach El Dorado?" Maybell leaned forward on the wooden bench and slapped the reins. "Giddy up you long-eared sons of Satan."

"With the wagon, I'd say a good six days. If we get lucky, maybe five."

Under cover of the chattering females, Maybell said, "You could do a lot worse, Keeper."

His horse shied as he jerked on the reins. "Don't go

getting no ideas. Nothing's going on."

"Well, that's evident. And why isn't there? It's way past time you settled down."

"I think I'll see what's up ahead." Throwing her a disgusted look, he galloped away.

He set a strong pace all day, not even stopping for the noonday meal, having no desire to listen to any more female chatter.

As they pushed forward, the weather grew steadily colder and the sky sullen. It was late afternoon when he spied a rising cloud of dust coming toward them.

CHAPTER 3

He galloped back to the wagon and reined in. "Riders coming. Dora, Juanita, get in the wagon. Mrs. O'Donnell, drop to the back and stay out of sight."

"You think it's trouble?" Mrs. O'Donnell's eyes sharpened and she straightened in the saddle. The horse sensed the change in its rider and sidled. Absently, she patted its neck.

"Prepare for the worst, hope for the best. Now get to the back." With reins and heels, he turned his horse to the front.

The women climbed into the covered wagon, skirts rustling.

Mrs. O'Donnell dropped to the back.

A moment later three men came into view. Keeper rode out to meet them, forcing the men to stop before they reached the wagon. The riders reined in, their horses throwing clods of dirt as their hooves dug into the earth, their legs straight and stiff.

"Gooday." He leaned forward in the saddle, one hand on the pommel in a casual pose. But if one looked closely, they'd note the other rested on his right gun.

"Gooday. What are you doing out in the middle of nowhere, mister?" The man in the middle wore black and had a silver band around his hat. His hand too lay casually on his gun. He looked to be in his thirties as did his companions. All had the hard-eyed look of gunslingers. The guns themselves were Smith and Wesson number three revolvers, the .44 caliber pistols that professionals often carried and Keeper had no doubt would come out of their holsters as easy as his did. Being top break revolvers, they could also be reloaded just as easily.

"The wife and I," he jerked his thumb in Maybell's direction, "are headed to Missouri to see her sister. You boys?"

"We got a job lined up outside of Wichita." He looked at the double six-guns on Keeper's hips. "What line of work you in, mister?"

"Oh, I'm just a farmer." He settled deeper into the saddle. "You boys?"

"Farmers one and all."

The man on Keeper's left snickered. His face was pockmarked and he had an edge to him that the other two didn't. He'd bear close watching. The man on the right had a nose, like Keeper's, that had been broken a time or too. He stared intently at Maybell. "Your wife looks familiar."

"I hear that a lot." Keeper's voice dry.

Two things happened at once. "Ouch, Juanita, you stepped on my foot." Dora screeched. A bear, downwind of them, came meandering over a low rise, saw them, stood on his hind legs roared and bulleted away.

That tore it.

Mrs. O'Donnell's mount bolted. Hauling on the reins, she got it under control before it was halfway around the wagon. It reared and her hat came off, blue-black hair cascading in magnificent disarray to her hips.

Riders' eyes grew hot. The shooter in the middle actually licked his lips. "Mister, you've been holding out on us. No point in keeping all those goodies for yourself."

Like lightning, Keeper's gun was out of his holster. "Don't come any closer." His voice deepened. His eyes narrowed.

The man in the middle spoke first. "There's three of us. One of you. The odds aren't in your favor."

"Maybe. Maybe not. But the one I take down will be you."

"Not if one of my partners get you first."

All three men had their hands on their guns. The horses, sensing the tension, were sidling including Keeper's mount. He tightened his grip on the reins and his bay settled, still tossing his head and snorting.

As if nature sensed death, the clouds darkened and mist drifted in, coating everything in ghostly white.

Keeper heard the click of a hammer and all hell broke loose. He twisted toward the man on the left and fired. The man slumped in the saddle. Lead flew.

The mules hee-hawed, bucked and took off. The women inside screaming. One of the men wheeled his horse toward the wagon, the prize that was getting away. A flash of silver flew through the air and landed in his shoulder. In slow motion, the rider fell off the horse and thudded onto the ground, the blade skewering him.

Astonishment jumped through Keeper's system. That knife could have come from only one person, Mrs. O'Donnell. Riding low in the saddle she went racing after the wagon.

A bullet so close it heated his ear brought him back to the business at hand. The center rider was the only one left. He and the rider drew at the same time. The mist rolled out as the bushwacker dropped from the saddle.

Keeper rode up to him, leaped off his horse and toed him over with his boot. The man's eyes were glazing over, a pool of crimson spreading on his shirt. "Who are you?" he gasped out, blood dribbling from the side of his mouth.

"Keeper Tyree."

"Keeper Tyree." There was disgust and disbelief in the rasp of his voice as his chest rose and fell. "Just my luck." He closed his eyes, drew his last breath and lay still.

The hombre with the pockmarked face lay dead. The one with the knife through his shoulder twitched and moaned on the ground. Keeper reached over and drew out the knife with a quick and brutal jerk. The man shrieked. "I need help."

"I'm not putting a bullet through you. That's all the help you're getting from me." He wiped the knife on his pants, stuck it in his belt and mounted his horse. He thumped the bay in the ribs and galloped after the wagon.

Racing around a bend, he pulled the bay to a stiff-legged halt. The wagon had stopped. Mrs. O'Donnell was bent over the wagon seat, the other women crowded round. The look on her face confirmed his worst fears. Dread coursed through him. "Maybell?"

"Yes."

"Damn." He took off his hat and hit the side of his leg. "Is she alive?"

"I can speak for myself." Maybell's voice reedy. Relief washed through Keeper. At least she wasn't dead.

"A bullet got me in the shoulder. Could have been worse."

"It needs to come out." Mrs. O'Donnell had her hand over the wound. "Juanita, tear me a strip off your petticoat to stop the bleeding. Betty Lou, gather tumbleweeds and start a fire. Dora, lay a blanket on the ground. Mr. Tyree—"

"I got her." He jumped off his horse, climbed onto the wagon, picked up Maybell as gently as he could and climbed back down.

"Never a dull moment, Maybell," he teased, ignoring the worry eating him.

"Just like El Paso." She gave him a tight-lipped grin.

"Except then you had the good sense not to get shot."

"That's true."

"You got some bug juice in the wagon?"

"For my shoulder or to drink?"

"Both."

Dora spread the blanket on the ground and a

pillow. He laid Maybell on it. "Get the whiskey, will you? And bring a canteen."

Dora nodded, raised her skirts and hurtled to the wagon. A moment later, back with both.

Mrs. O'Donnell shouldered him aside. "I'll take it from here."

"I believe this is yours." He handed her the knife. "You have hidden talents, Mrs. O'Donnell."

"I don't like guns. Is he still alive?" She stared at a splash of blood on the handle.

"Don't know. Don't care."

"What about the other two?"

"Dead."

Her face went from pasty to stark white. "I guess those stories about you aren't exaggerated after all."

"Not hardly." His voice rough, his expression hard.

She handed the knife back. "Would you clean and sterilize it please?"

He poured whiskey over it and handed it back. Gently she cut away the shoulder of Maybell's dress then cleaned it with a damp strip from Juanita's petticoat.

His bones creaked in protest as he kneeled down then clasped Maybell in his arms and handed her a flask. "Drink up. I think you're going to need it." He looked at Mrs. O'Donnell. "Are you sure you don't want me to do this?"

"If you could do it with a gun, I wouldn't hesitate. As it is, I'll handle this." There wasn't a drop of color in her face, but determination rode in her voice and resolve sparked in her eyes.

"Have at it."

"Hold her down."

"That won't be necessary," Maybell protested as white as Mrs. O'Donnell.

Mrs. O'Donnell's gaze met Keeper's. He nodded and got a grip on Maybell.

As gently as possible, Mrs. O'Donnell probed the wound with her knife. "Tell me about El Paso, Maybell."

"Well, we—" She screamed as the knife dug in.

Mrs. O'Donnell probed torn flesh. Maybell screamed again. Mrs. O'Donnell sliced deeper, worked the knife around. She bit her lip, thrust and flipped out the bullet. Her breath rattling in harsh gasps, she threw the knife on the ground, poured whiskey over the wound and started to bandage it.

Maybell passed out.

With brisk movements, Keeper's employer finished cleaning and bandaging the wound then leaned back on her heels and with the back of her hand wiped her damp brow.

Keeper passed her the flask.

"Just this once." She took a long, deep swallow and came up coughing, but regained some color.

"You have a steady hand." A leg bent in front of him, he leaned forward to study her work.

"Thank you."

The women who'd hovered in the background gathered round and began thanking her.

"I'll take another swig of that." Her face pasty and pale, Maybell—who'd regained consciousness—lifted her head.

Keeper bolstered her up and held the flask for her. She took a healthy gulp. A little color came into her face.

"Why the hell didn't you get down?" Keeper demanded as he eased her back on the ground. "You think you're bullet proof?" Now that the worst was over, nerves exploded.

"Mr. Tyree, she's been through enough without you yelling at her."

"I'm hardly yelling." His eyebrows drew together and his jaw clenched.

Maybell held up her good hand in a stop-arguing gesture. "He's right. It was stupid of me. Keeper, next time you draw your gun I'll be burrowing under the seat."

"Very funny," he grumbled. He took a healthy swig and his world made an effort to settle. "We'll camp here for the night. I'll see to the horses. Let's get the fire built up, and some coffee and vittles on. I'm going to do some hunting."

He pushed up and strode away from camp toward a grove of trees. Twenty or so minutes later he came back with a couple of rabbits, he'd shot. Mrs. O'Donnell reached for them. With a shy smile, Juanita held out her hand. "You've done your fair share today. I'll take care of these."

"Thank you, Juanita."

"You're welcome." The girl was on the plain side, but when she smiled her whole face lit up.

"Anything I can do to help?" Dark circles under

her eyes, Mrs. O'Donnell stretched. Still, being faced with someone else's problems had lessened the look of strain that dogged her. Formed fine lines around her eyes and kept her lips thin and tight. He glanced down and caught Maybell watching him, a knowing look on her face. Everyone gave him a bewildered glance when he shook his head, threw up his hands and stalked off.

Settled, he came back as the sky met the earth in a fuse of color then turned to ink. A full moon popped out, along with a handful of stars. Orange fire jumped, crackled and warmed. The scent of roasting hare had his stomach gurgling. Two rabbits didn't go that far among six people, but when Maybell threw in more of their canned items and Mrs. O'Donnell did the same, he declared it a feast.

The fire lighting her features, Mrs. O'Donnell helped Maybell to a sitting position and filled a plate for her. She needed the busy, the fussing after someone he realized. And wondered, not for the first time, how she could leave her little girl to search for vengeance.

He toed a pebble with his boot. It wasn't his place to judge. He'd never had a child, never expected to, so he had no idea the workings of mind and heart when someone born of your blood and bone was ripped violently from you. Still and all she had to move on. That little girl needed her momma.

He took a slug of his coffee, waited till she sat down with her own plate and went and sat beside her. The other women laughing and talking quietly amongst themselves in the background. The fire crackling.

"That was some fine knife throwing today."

"Thank you, Mr. Tyree."

"Who taught you to throw like that?"

"My brother and I used to have knife throwing contests when we were growing up. The old oak behind the house got pretty carved up." Her face softened and she smiled at the memory. Something in Keeper swelled, warmed and settled. He was in trouble and he knew it.

"You know everyone calls me either Keeper or Tyree. I would be pleased if you would as well."

She set her coffee on the ground and holding her plate with one hand, held the other out to him. "Cathleen."

He took it and once again, felt the warmth with a hint of soft and a touch of firm. Not quite rough, but not cossetted either. Hands that worked and worked hard. He realized he was still holding it when she tugged at it. He let go and for a moment, just stared at her blankly.

A high-pitched scream had him on his feet and pivoting.

CHAPTER 4

The hombre Cathleen had knifed stood at the edge of the camp, his shirt dark with blood, his barker drawn, swaying on his feet.

"Get down," Keeper hollered.

Cathleen threw herself on the ground. Maybell scooted into the shadows and the other women scrambled out of the firelight and into the dark.

A hammer clicked, loud in the quiet.

Keeper's gun appeared like lightning from his holster. His blood rushing, his head cool, he fired. The barker dropped from the would-be shooter's fingers and he crumpled to his knees then landed face down beside the fire, jostling it enough that sparks flew in the sky several landing on his shirt as they fell, but he never moved.

Keeper kicked him over. The man dead alright. How he'd ever managed to get on his horse and ride after them was anybody's guess. He gave himself a mental kick in the pants. He should have put a bullet in him back there and then instead of chancing anyone else getting hurt. He must be getting soft...or old.

The women gathered around.

"Is he dead?" Dora asked.

"He's dead alright." Keeper's voice gritty, his face hard.

She bent down and riffled his vest pockets, pulling out several double eagles. With a swish of skirts, she stood. "For the cookie jar."

"What is it with women and cookie jars?" He shook his head, grabbed the bushwacker by the boots and hauled him out of camp.

When he got back, he seized his flask, poured a healthy amount into his cup then passed the flask around. Cathleen was the only one to decline. He lifted his cup to her. "Life certainly isn't dull around you." Then downed the contents.

~*~

The rich fragrant smell of fresh perked coffee woke him, quickly followed by the usual aches and pains that plagued him.

He was getting too old for jaunting all over the countryside. Maybe it was time to hang up his spurs. Over the years he'd built up a decent nest egg. Unlike the women and their cookie jars, he kept his under a loose floorboard in his room. When moving from town to town, he kept it in his handmade boots, that had a special lining to keep his money in. The only way anyone would get to it is if they killed him. In that case, his money would probably be buried with him. He carried paper currency, lighter than coins, when on the move. As soon as he lighted in a town, he changed it out for double eagles. Even if the money in circulation got to be worthless, gold was gold.

He stretched, tugged on his boots with the padding of currency in the lining, and followed his nose to the coffeepot. A couple of gulps of the hot liquid and his head cleared.

After breakfast they bedded Maybell in the back of the wagon and continued their journey. Cathleen clucked over Maybell as if she were a hen with one chick.

If she chafed from the delay, to find Pardee, she neither said nor showed it. He admired her for it. Though occasionally he glimpsed a flat, frozen look in her eyes when she gazed at the horizon.

He'd felt the bone hard desire for revenge before and knew how it ate at a person until it was quenched. Unfortunately, he also knew that the quenching took a bit of one's soul with it. Once again, he reminded himself his job was finding Pardee, not worrying about Mrs. O'Donnell's soul. Not worrying about her period. Unfortunately, it seemed he had to remind himself of that too often for his comfort as they made their way to El Dorado.

They were two days from their destination when disaster struck, again. He'd hobbled the mules away from the campsite where they could graze on brown dead grass and a few hardy green shoots trying to pop through for spring.

Bedded down by a stream and grove of trees, Keeper sat straight up in the dark when he heard one of the mule's scream followed by the snarls of a wild cat.

Dawn had yet to break through the horizon, the animals' shapes shadowy as the mule desperately fought for his life, hindered by the hobble. Cursing, Keeper ran forward but knew it was too late. He raised his gun and took down the puma.

The mule, on the ground, thrashed and brayed.

The women came running as dawn broke, loosening a watery sun on a still gray sky. Cathleen dropped to her knees beside the mule. She murmured words of comfort and stroked the red-streaked neck.

"Mrs. O'Donnell."

She ignored him, just kept murmuring to the mule who had quieted and lay quivering.

"Cathleen."

Finally, she looked at him.

"He's too badly hurt and he's suffering. Step away."

Maybell, who had climbed out of the wagon, put her good hand on Cathleen's shoulder. "Come on, honey, let Keeper take care of this."

She pushed to her feet. Her movements stiff as if her joints hurt her. She brushed past without looking at him.

"Damn." He waited till she was out of sight then shot the mule. He sighed. The woman cared too much. No wonder the loss of her son had driven her half-mad. He looked at the puma. It was scrawny and looked half-starved. It had to be hungry to attack an animal this close to camp. The buzzards would take care of clean up.

"Hell of a mess." He stared at the two carcasses then strode back to camp.

The women huddled up against the wagon.

Cathleen had regained her composure, emotion once more wiped from her face. "What do we do now?"

"One mule can't pull this wagon. We'll have to hook up your horse."

"What about your horse?"

"Forget it." His voice flat, he pokered-up.

She tapped her toe and mulled it over. "Since I'm riding in the wagon to keep an eye on Maybell, I guess it makes sense." She turned away.

"Dang beatenest woman I've ever met," he muttered, reaching for his hat only to realize he wasn't wearing one. Weeping over a mule one moment, giving him sass the next.

"Mr. Tyree?"

He whirled around to see Juanita at his elbow. "Should I start breakfast?" The breaking sun highlighted freckles on her small plain face.

"That's a great idea."

"I like her." Then she too disappeared into the wagon.

He threw his hands in the air, irritated to realize he'd spoke out loud.

After a breakfast of strong coffee, oatmeal and hardtack, he put Cathleen's confused horse in the traces next to the mule. First it balked then reared. At that point, the mule began to bray and buck. He grabbed the halters of the two nervous animals and bellowed, "Cathleen. Calm down your cayuse."

She climbed down and hurried to her horse, where

she stroked and soothed her. "This isn't your normal job is it, girl?

"What do you want me to do?" she asked Keeper still concentrating on the horse.

The sun chose that moment to drift from behind a wispy white cloud, coating Cathleen and her horse in a sheen of gold, giving her an unworldly beauty that both drew him and made him uneasy. He shifted in his saddle.

"Well?" She turned to him, her eyes narrowed.

The moment passed and he once more faced the cantankerous female he was more used to and comfortable with. "Just lead her for a few minutes to get her used to the new commands. If she settles down so will the mule. Dora, let's get them moving."

"Whatever you say, handsome." Dora clicked the reins.

Keeper didn't miss Cathleen's eyeroll and grinned. A hand on her mare's bridle, they set off with Cathleen tromping beside the horse. It took 'em a good half hour before the mare settled into the trace. Satisfied the horse had calmed, Cathleen climbed up on the wagon with Dora.

"Honey, you do have a way with animals." Skirts rustling, Dora scooted over to make room for Cathleen as she rolled her hips on the hard, wooden seat. No doubt looking for a comfortable spot

"And you have a way with men." Cathleen's voice dry.

"I surely do, honey. I surely do. All you got to do is appeal to their manhood. Stroke it a bit if you know what I mean." She gave a loud guffaw and elbowed Cathleen in the ribs.

This time, Keeper rolled his eyes. He wasn't easily embarrassed, but if this conversation kept up, he would be.

He kicked his horse in the ribs and it galloped away from the wagon but not before he heard Cathleen respond, "I'm beginning to." His ears burning, he kept the horse at a fast pace, till he rounded a bend and hauled his horse to a stiff-legged halt, rubbing his eyes, not quite believing what lay across the trail. "Whoa." Then, "Well, I'll be damned. Mister, how the hell did that happen?"

CHAPTER 5

A huge uprooted oak lay across a covered wagon. Thick, rough-barked branches with pale green leaves trying to bud pushed through the canvas and lay scattered on the ground. A stoop-shouldered man stood beside the broken vehicle, holding a rifle at an awkward angle.

Not much angered Keeper more than a gun pointed at him by someone who had no idea how to use it.

Hands on his saddle pommel, he growled, "Put that damn thing away. I mean you no harm."

The man looked at the rifle, through spectacles that emphasized blurry blue eyes, as if seeing it for the first time. "Oh, sorry." He hastily lowered it to the ground, barrel first, causing Keeper to wince at the dirt and dry leaves going into the muzzle.

"What happened here?"

"The tree fell in the middle of the night. Guess, the roots loosened." He gave a helpless shrug and ran thin fingers through tousled hair.

"And your horses or mules?" Keeper looked around but didn't see any signs of them.

"They ran off when the tree crashed."

"Didn't you hobble them?" Though that sure hadn't helped his any, he reflected wryly.

"No. I guess I should have."

"Where you headed?"

"El Dorado. Going to set up a law office there."

Keeper grunted. The answer didn't surprise him. The awkward way he held the rifle, the spectacles and the general look of helplessness, all shouted bookworm. Not that he had a problem with folks that kept their nose in a book, they just had no business in the raw, violent West.

He unwound one of his canteens from the saddle pommel and tossed it to the stranger. "I'm heading that way. It'll be a couple of days but I'll send someone back to help."

They were short on mules and horses, the wagon wouldn't hold more than it had now and they didn't need another mouth to feed.

The man gave a nod, his expression resigned. "Any help is appreciated, of course."

"Pa." A little tow-headed boy who appeared to be about five or six came running out of the trees.

"Well, hell." Resignation weighed down his shoulders. He could leave a man with no qualms, but not a child. Wasn't there an old tale about a pied piper? That's what he was beginning to feel like. He'd take a shootout with a bullet-spraying hombre any day of the week in place of a passel of women and children, but a man wasn't a man if he didn't do his duty.

He straightened his shoulders, his voice gruff. "Toss the lad up. You can come with me."

Behind the thick lenses the man's watery eyes widened. "Just a moment, let me grab my books."

"Your books? That's what you're taking with you?"

"My law books." He was back a few minutes later with several well-worn volumes strapped to his back. He lifted his son in his arms and tossed him up behind Keeper. Gratitude made his myopic eyes shine. "I don't know how to thank you."

"Ain't doing it for you." Doing his duty always aggravated him and made his voice raspier, like crunchy gravel under a boot.

"But you are doing it. And even before you saw the boy, you left me one of your canteens."

"Don't make more of it than it is."

"I can see you don't like to be thanked, Mr.—" He held out his hand.

"Tyree. Keeper Tyree." He shook the proffered, freshly blistered, hand. A hand unused to manual labor. Still the fellow had an honest face. Lord knows what he was doing out West. The men Keeper knew could chew him up and spit him out.

"Mr. Tyree, I'm Ezekiel Jones and this is Jacob."

"Jacob." Keeper shook the boy's hand.

"Mr. Tyree."

"Just call me Keeper. Everyone else does."

"Your mom must have loved you a lot." Blue eyes without the wateriness of their father's looked up at him.

His name always elicited comments, especially among the younkers. He liked kids. They were forthright, without adult bias. If he had taken a different path, he would have gladly had a dozen of his own.

"Yes, she did. You're a smart lad. Now we better get going."

He wheeled his horse and started back toward the rest of his party.

"Mr. Tyree, aren't we heading in the wrong direction?" Ezekiel trotted beside him.

"Watch how you carry that rifle," Keeper barked as the barrel angled in his direction.

"Oh, sorry."

"The wagon's back this way."

"You've got a wagon?"

He didn't bother with an answer. It was too damn complicated. He just kept the horse at a trot.

An hour later, they entered camp. Keeper had to give Ezekiel his due. Even though he was soaked in sweat and wheezing, he'd kept up, making no complaints about the pace. It raised him several notches in Keeper's opinion. Whiners got on his nerves. He'd just as soon shoot them as listen to them.

He came to a halt beside the wagon.

"Whoa." Dora hauled on the reins and stopped the wagon. The women came spilling out, surrounding a befuddled-looking Ezekiel. They encircled him, hurling questions. Even Maybell stuck her head out of the wagon then with awkward movements, climbed out.

"Who ya got there, Keeper?"

"Look at that darling little boy."

"What's your name, sweetheart?"

Sounded like a hive of bees droning, Keeper thought, resigned to the questions and the female-flutterings.

He glanced at Cathleen. She gazed at the little boy, a rare smile on her face. One that not only lifted her lips but shone out of her eyes. As if drawn, she took two steps forward and held out her arms. He dropped the boy into them. She held him for a moment then loosened her hands till they lay lightly on his shoulders. "I'm Cathleen. Who are you?"

"Jacob Jones." The boy beamed back, entranced.

Her smile had that affect. Keeper'd only caught a piece of it, but still it sent a tingle through him right down to his booted toes.

"I'm here with my dad. We are going to El Dorado where my dad's going to practice law."

All eyes swiveled to Ezekiel. The women oohed and aahed.

If Ezekiel thought it was strange to be surrounded by ladies of the evening, he gave no notice. Maybe he wasn't aware of their calling. More like he wasn't aware of them at all, his attention, no his entire being, focused on Cathleen. Ezekiel's mouth hung open. Color rushed to his face.

What kind of growed man blushed anyhow?

Ezekiel ran his fingers through unruly brown hair, trying to tame it. And even through the spectacles, he had a dazed—more dazed than Keeper had previously seen—expression. He took a few stumbling steps forward and reached for Cathleen's hand and shook it. "I'm Ezekiel Jones, ma'am."

He didn't even have the decency to drop it. Just kept holding it.

The other ladies poked each other and tittered.

Cathleen gently extracted her hand.

He looked from one to the other. His stomach knotted. His lips puckered like he'd bit into something sour. Her face didn't have the look of ice-ready-to-crack like it did when she gazed at him. Nor did her eyes burn like live coals ignited by vengeance.

Instead, her gaze warm, alive and curious.

He looked at Ezekiel and tried to see him through her eyes. Young, younger than he anyway. Probably thirty or thereabouts. Handsome in a tousled way and well-educated. Nothing like himself, a gunslinger on the bad side of forty, arthritic, hard-edged. No school learning to speak of.

To his surprise a sigh escaped his lips.

He shifted in his saddle and glanced over at Maybell who stared steadily back, her eyebrows arched, wearing a what-are-you-going-to-do-about-it expression.

He swung out of the saddle. While everyone else gathered around Ezekiel and the boy, she marched straight to him and stopped in front of him, her good hand on her hip. "Well?"

"A tree took out his wagon."

Before he could say more, she interrupted. "That's not what I'm asking and you know it."

He led his horse to a clear-flowing stream he'd spied nearby. Maybell on his heels.

After the horses were watered, they could still get

in better than a half day of travel. The stream was the one piece of luck they'd had in this God-awful day.

"I have no idea what you are talking about."

"You've got your share of faults, Keeper, that's the God's honest truth, but lying to anyone, yourself included ain't one of them." She stood tapping her toe.

"Your shoulder must be bothering you, Maybell. You ain't normally this testy."

"Keeper, we go way back. We had a few good times."

"We did that." He picked up a stone and threw it up and down in the air then tossed it into the stream where it rippled a few times then sank.

"And after that we became friends."

"Won't argue that either."

"Then I hope you won't mind some plain speaking."

"Maybell, you don't know any other way." And wished he had the heart to tell her to mind her own business.

"Cathleen is the best thing that ever happened to you. Don't let her get away."

"That woman is not mine. Our relationship is strictly business."

"More fool you then."

"She wouldn't be interested in an old gunslinger. She's more the type that would prefer an up-and-coming lawyer. Even if he couldn't find his way out of a cathouse at night."

She gave an unexpected laugh then grew serious. "You talk like you're a hundred years old. You're a man still in his prime. Plenty of the girls have told me that." She gave him a onceover that made him give an embarrassed snort.

She continued, "Keeper, you're ugly as an old buffalo but you can charm the leaves off the trees when you set your mind to it. There's something down right attractive in that ugliness."

"I don't know if I've been complimented or insulted."

"You'll know when I've insulted you. I've never known you to delude yourself before. You've picked a heck of a time to start." With a swish of skirts, she strode away.

He slapped his hat against his thigh. "Well hell."

~*~

"Look at that eagle!"

Jacob, riding beside Dora, jumped up on the wagon seat and pointed at the great bird, wings spread wide, floating in a sky as bright and caerulean as a field of blue-bonnets. The boy enlivened the tedium of the remainder of the days that it took them to get to El Dorado. The women cossetted both he and his father. To his credit Ezekiel never inquired into the women's profession or what they were doing on the trail. Keeper wouldn't be surprised if they didn't tell him of their own accord. They were relaxed around him and took him at face value as he did them.

Still, Keeper wished Ezekiel would spread his earnest, schoolboy charm around all the women instead of honing it on Cathleen. His brows drew together and his stomach turned, like the time he'd ate bad meat at a small cafe in Wichita, as Ezekiel and Cathleen walked beside the wagon. He nearly reeled in his saddle when he heard her laugh. A rusty sound with rich overtones. Made him think of silk sheets he'd slept on in St. Louie and fine whiskey he'd drank in the same place. He reined himself in, he had no business thinking those things about a good, God-fearing woman. Still and all, he'd have to be gelded not to think of 'em. Maybe it was time to get a woman. He looked speculatively at Dora who at that moment looked over her shoulder, caught his eye and winked.

He glanced again at Cathleen and Ezekiel and found Cathleen watching him too. Okay, maybe not Dora.

He thumped his heels against his stallion. The big bay threw up his head, snorted and broke into a gallop, his hooves tearing at the brown stubs of grass under his heels. They pulled ahead of the wagon and galloped up the slope.

The horse came to a stiff-legged halt as Keeper reined him in. Below lay the bustling town of El Dorado. Wooden buildings lined winding streets. One cowboy pushed another through the swinging doors of a saloon, where he landed on his butt in the dusty street. He wiped his hands on his pants and charged back in. Keeper grinned and shook his head. A typical rough and ready Western town.

He waited till the wagon pulled alongside then yelled, "Maybell, hie yourself out of that wagon and show me where we are headed."

A clambering sounded from the wagon like a couple of tin cups had fallen from the makeshift cupboard inside and rolled across the floor. Ezekiel reached up a helping hand as Maybell lowered herself off the back of the wagon.

"Are we there?"

"As near as dammit." His lips flashed up in a grin. His hands on the pommel, he raised himself in the saddle then settled back into it.

She grabbed her skirt with her free hand and hurried up beside him, a smile of pride on her plump features.

"Which one's yours?" He settled back in the saddle.

She covered her eyes with her hand and squinted into the sun. Then pointed, "That one at the end."

"That big, three story pink one at the outskirts of town with the sun reflecting off the copper roof of a bay window?"

"That's it." Her chest swelled.

A clearly awesome sight.

He chewed on a smile. He'd have bet the small fortune in his boots that the pink monstrosity at the end of the road was Maybell's when he sighted it.

"I owe you for getting us here, Keeper. She squeezed his leg above his boot. "And if I didn't have so much respect for your woman back there." She jerked her head in the direction of Cathleen who was coming around the wagon. "I'd show you just how much I appreciate what you've done for us."

He stiffened in the saddle, inadvertently jerking on the reins at the same time causing his horse to dance backwards, Ezekiel barely getting out of the way of the stallion's hooves while getting a mouthful of cornhusk-colored tail in his mouth. Even Maybell took a hasty step back.

"Not mine and two different issues entirely. He reined in his dancing stallion. "Let's go see your new place."

Maybell reached around and untied her sling, rolled her sore shoulder and approached the front of the wagon. "Move over, Dora, I'm taking the reins."

Before he could swing out of the saddle to help her, Ezekiel hurried forward, pushing his glasses, that had slipped down, up to the bridge of his nose. "Let me help you, Maybell. Are you sure you're up to this?"

"I'm tough as a chicken's claw, young man."

"Of course, you are." He gave her a charming smile.

Keeper rolled his eyes.

Ezekiel boosted her up and blushed to his hairline when his hands came in contact with her wide bottom.

Keeper grinned.

Cathleen glared at him.

"I like your laugh much better than I do your frown. It reminds me of a school marm I had as a young'un that was always rapping my knuckles."

The remark surprised a reluctant chuckle. "Somehow I can't help thinking those knuckle rappings were well-deserved."

"I won't argue that. Doesn't mean I liked it one whit better."

"I can't say that I blame you."

For a rare moment they smiled at each other, in accord.

"Let's go see my house." Maybell's voice boomed, breaking the moment.

Keeper tipped his hat and moved his horse forward.

"Here, Jacob. You crack the whip," Maybell directed the boy, hanging on the edge of the seat.

"I don't want to hurt the animals."

"You don't actually hit them with it. You crack it in the air. It's the noise that gets them going. Here, you hold the reins and I'll show you."

The whip cracked as Keeper's mount shot forward, the wagon rattling behind him. Betty Lou and Juanita had hopped out of the wagon too, electing to walk so they could get a better view of their new home and new town.

On the outskirts, Keeper reined in and waited. Cowboys strolled down the town's wooden sidewalks. Town ladies bustled in and out of the café and mercantile. Horses stomped and swished their tails where they were tied next to the sidewalk.

The wagon came rolling up and kept going. "What are you waiting for, Keeper?" Maybell bellowed.

Jacob leaned over and grinned at him.

The women and Ezekiel strode behind, all grinning from ear to ear. As they strode through town, behind the wagon, Keeper trotted beside them, one hand on the reins, one on his thigh.

People on the sidewalk stopped and stared openly. Men came tumbling out of the saloons. One of the cowboys, waving a bottle at them, spied Cathleen and came stumbling toward her.

"Sweetheart, where have you been all my life. None of my friends look nearly this good in pants." His friends guffawed. He made a grab for her. Ezekiel stepped forward. "Leave the lady alone."

The man took a wild swing and with more luck than science knocked Ezekiel to the ground. His glasses hung from one ear as he picked himself up to a sitting position.

His jaw like granite, his ears thrumming, Keeper nudged his horse between the drunken cowboy and Cathleen and Ezekiel.

"Hey." The drunk raised his whiskey bottle and before he could swing it, Keeper shot it out of his hand. Shattered glass glittered like diamonds in the western sun as they fell like rain onto the dirt street.

Wide-eyed, Jacob peeked around the wagon as his dad picked himself up and put his specs back on, and Cathleen took her hat off and shook broken shards off of it.

"Mister, I'm going to give you to the count of three to offer this lady an apology and then take yourself off and out of my sight. If you haven't done it by three, I'm going to put a hole in you."

"Sorry, ma'am." He doffed his hat and staggered off before Keeper started to count.

Jacob jumped from the wagon and ran to Keeper. "Gosh, Mr. Tyree, that was sure something. Would you teach me to shoot?" His face turned up, hero worship shone in his eyes. Belatedly, he turned to his dad who was dusting himself off. "Are you okay, Dad?"

"I'm fine, Jacob." His face brick red, mortification slumped his shoulders and twisted his lips.

Keeper leaned down in his saddle. "Son, anyone can handle a gun. It takes a man of intelligence and book learning to beat someone in a court of law. Not to mention stand up for a lady when the odds aren't in his favor."

"What does that mean?" Confusion chased across his young face.

"It means in the long run your dad is the one who is going to stand up for what's right and make a difference in this world. You'd be better off with book learning like your dad." He straightened in the saddle. "Still every man needs to be able to defend himself. If your dad approves, I'll teach you the basics."

"Gosh, thank you, Mr. Tyree." He spun to his dad. "You don't mind, do you?"

His self-esteem restored, Ezekiel threw a grateful look at Keeper. "If you are going to learn the basics then it should be from the best. Maybe Mr. Tyree would give me a few pointers too."

Keeper's respect for Ezekiel went up another notch. A real man admitted when he needed help and didn't make excuses for it.

"If time allows."

His gaze shifted to Cathleen. A jolt shot through him.

She watched him with an expression he couldn't quite read. Since the odd assemblage of folks that joined them had taken them off track in search of

Pardee, she'd lost that brittle self-destruct look that shone in her eyes. He still sensed an impatience, a feverishness about her to get on with what they'd planned but it was honed, controlled.

"Show's over folks. Let's move it." Maybell's voice boomed. The whip cracked and the unevenly yoked animals trotted forward. Wood groaned as the wagon jerked then rolled.

Folks on the sidewalk that had been gawking at the fight, now hustled along with them. No doubt, expecting more entertainment. When they reached the end of the road and pulled in front of the huge pink monstrosity, Maybell lowered herself from the wagon. She turned to the crowd. "We'll be open for business in a month, folks. There will be a café. A drinking establishment and a place for gent's entertainment if you get my drift." She gave a big wink.

Many of the men clapped. The women gave gasps and with a lift of skirts hurried away, except for one or two who wore a look of mild interest.

Maybell clapped her hands together. "Boys, when we open you are welcome. But know this. When you come through my doors you better be cleaned and well-behaved or you'll find yourself out on the streets faster than you can down a whiskey."

A cowboy who'd been hooting when the drunk accosted Cathleen shouted out, "I ain't taking a bath for no whore."

"Then take one for us, Marty." One of his witty friends guffawed.

Anger rushed fast and hard through Keeper's system. No man had a right to talk to a woman that way, no matter their calling. Not to mention he hadn't cooled down from that idiot accosting Cathleen. Riled up, he swung off his horse, strode to the mouthy cowboy, jerked him around and put his fist right between the hombre's eyes. The other men got out of the way as the cowboy fell to the ground like a felled tree.

"Anyone else got anything to say about these women?" Still heated up, he turned in a slow circle his gaze missing no one.

The onlookers shuffled their feet and began to back away. A few tipped their hats as they left.

Though the western sun shone bright, a chill lingered in the air and nipped at Keeper's temper. Either that or flattening the loudmouth had taken care of the fire inside him that even had his ears hot. He rubbed his hands together, in a much better mood. "Let's see your place, Maybell."

Chattering, the women hustled inside. Cathleen hung back. "I underestimated you."

"Oh?"

"You're every bit as hard and tough as I heard." Her eyes held no condemnation and again something sparked in them that he couldn't quite read.

"And you always keep me off balance." The words were out before he could recall them. He made it a point never to show weakness with man or woman. And being off balance hardly showed strength.

A small smile came and went on her features and

her eyes twinkled. "Good." She swept past him, trotted up the porch steps and disappeared into the cavernous building.

"Women." He threw his hands in the air.

Ezekiel who'd come up behind him nodded in agreement, staring at the doorway Cathleen had disappeared through. "Wondrous creatures, but who knows what goes on in their minds."

For once in perfect accord with the book learner, he slapped him on the back. "If they get that bar set up tonight, I'll buy you a drink."

Ezekiel winced at the thump that nearly sent him sprawling. "Thanks, I'll take you up on that." Then added, his voice wistful, "She's awfully pretty."

"That we agree on." Keeper shoved past him into the house.

Everyone stood in a huge drafty entryway chattering at once. Jacob ran down the hall, opening and closing doors.

"That chandelier is gorgeous." Dora pointed overhead.

Hands in pockets, Keeper rocked on his heels and studied it. A candelabra with over forty candles in pearl cups with tear-drop prisms hanging beneath them hung from the center of the curly-cued ceiling. "You're going to need a housekeeper, Maybell."

"Or two. It's eye-catching for sure, but it's going to need a day's worth of cleaning." She sneezed as dust motes floated her way.

"Come on." She pulled a white-laced handkerchief out of the bosom of her dress, blew her nose and motioned them forward.

The next door she opened led into a wide parlor. The walls were a drab yellow. Dust covers were thrown over sofas, tables and a piano that sat in the corner. A black wool carpet with overblown red roses covered the floor.

"Needs a new coat of paint." Maybell noted, staring at dirty walls. Then moved on.

"This will be the café. We'll have a door made on the outside. Juanita, there's a kitchen that sets behind this room." She pointed to a doorway. Juanita bulleted in and squealed in delight.

"Sounds like the kitchen meets with her approval." Betty Lou grinned.

Maybell stepped out and opened the next door. "This will be the saloon. It will also have an outside entrance."

"Why the outside entrance?" Cathleen asked as she looked around.

"I want the townsfolk, not just randy cowboys."

Cathleen tried to school her face to hide the skepticism.

"I intend to throw up a barrier in the front between the gentlemen's house and the other side that will offer accommodation for the townspeople. I'll build a separate veranda along the side. You'll see." She dipped and lifted her chin in Cathleen's direction.

"You've convinced me." Cathleen gave her a warm smile that had a strange effect on Keeper's knees. Arthritis he told himself.

"And what's this room?" Jacob asked, opening the

next.

"Why that's your daddy's law office if he wants it."

"What's that?" Ezekiel's head shot up and he blinked.

"You got an office yet? A place to stay?"

"Well, err, no."

"I'm going to convert the third-floor attic into bedrooms and sitting rooms for those that want it. There will be an outside entrance there too so they don't go through the girls' area." She nodded at Jacob who'd wandered back into the hall and gone back to poking his head into doorways. "The boy won't be exposed to anything he shouldn't. Once we're open for business that part of the building will be off limits to him."

"I don't know what to say." Ezekiel looked more befuddled than usual, his eyes suspiciously bright.

"Say yes or no."

"Yes." To everyone's surprise he took two hasty steps forward, grabbed Maybell and gave her a sound buss on the cheek, causing the girls to titter and even Keeper to break into a grin.

Maybell waved him off, though, she wore a pleased expression. "I won't charge you much until you get on your feet and get your clientele built up."

"I'm sure you'll be fair."

"You can count on it."

"If you're renting rooms, you're going to want your steps indoors. No one is going to want to climb three flights in bad weather." Hands in pockets, Keeper rocked on his heels.

Maybell tapped her fingers against her cheek, her forehead wrinkled. "You're right. Details that can be worked out."

"Where will we be working?" Dora asked.

A blush rose in both Cathleen's and Ezekiel's faces. Keeper grinned again.

"There's ten bedrooms upstairs. I look for them to fill up quickly so go pick out which ones you want."

Juanita looked after the girls uncertainly.

"You'll be up on the renters' floor, as soon as we get some dividing walls thrown up. For now, pick yourself out a bedroom on the second floor."

Skirts hiked, Juanita went flying after the others, their shoes clattering on the dusty mahogany stairs.

"Where's your room?" Cathleen asked.

"I've got a suite on the other side of the hall. It's a nice set up, bedroom, office and sitting room."

"You know this is going to cost you a small fortune."

"I've been saving a long time. I can handle it. Besides it's an investment."

"You're going to make some carpenter a happy man." Keeper tapped his hat against his leg. "How'd you find this place anyway?"

"Remember, One-eyed Sally?"

"One-eyed Sal. Of course."

"She built this place."

"Where's she now?"

"Back East. She'd barely opened when a drunken cowboy beat one of her girls to death. Weren't too much more than a child. Sal loved her like her own.

She just didn't have any heart left for this business after that happened and offered to sell it to me."

Silence fell. He and most of his acquaintance didn't think past a bought moment of pleasure to the hardship that faced these women. No wonder some grew cold and hard.

A look of profound sadness settled over Cathleen's face before she straightened her shoulders and cleared her throat. "I wish you all the best." She held out her hand to Maybell, then turned to Keeper. "After the wagon is unloaded, we best be moving on. My horse won't know what to do with a saddle on her back again." She laughed.

"You can't." Ezekiel looked like he'd been gut shot.

"Stay the night. Help us celebrate," Maybell coaxed. "I saw a café—we're going to give them competition—on the main street of town. We'll go out to eat. My treat."

Cathleen looked uncertain, clearly wanting to get on the road, but not knowing how to gracefully bow out from the invite.

"Please." Ezekiel wore a charming smile. "Plus, Jacob and I need an hour or so of Mr. Tyree's time for that gun lesson."

"You're going to need more than an hour but an hour is what you're going to get." Tyree rocked on his heels, his hands in his back pockets.

She opened her mouth then closed it. Her shoulders sagged "Alright." Frustration shone from her eyes for a moment before masked.

"Great." Ezekiel beamed and rubbed his hands

together.

"Wonderful." Maybell smiled, hands on hips.

"Ezekiel, let's get the wagon unloaded. Then I'll give you two that lesson." Keeper strode out then trotted down the porch steps, his boot heels clicking on the wooden planks, heading for the wagon.

"Come on, Jacob," Ezekiel called out and followed Keeper outside.

It took several trips that had Keeper's arthritis grumbling and even in the chill air, sweat running down his back, but they got it done. The women moved the lighter items which helped considerably thought Keeper as the three of them rode out of town, Ezekiel and Jacob doubled up on Cathleen's roan.

Tomorrow morning, he could leave with a clear conscience though he wished there was a man around who could handle a gun. Hence the lessons.

A tumbleweed blew by, causing Cathleen's roan to skitter to her right, nearly unseating Ezekiel.

"Lor' save us," Keeper muttered, shaking his head.

Ezekiel gave him an apologetic smile and got his horse under control.

"What did you say, Mr. Tyree?" Jacob threw him a curious look, swaying with the horse's movements.

"Nothing, son." He pointed to an oak up ahead. "We'll practice there." The tree's stately branches stretched out in a near perfect circle. Come summer, dark green, lobed leaves would blanket it in emerald glory. Seemed a shame to shoot off that perfect symmetry, but he didn't have tin cans and he didn't believe in taking a life, of man or beast, without cause.

He reined in and swung out of the saddle.

Ezekiel managed to get down without tripping and Jacob jumped to the ground landing in a squatting position on his feet then pushed upward.

They strode toward the tree.

"You got any other guns, Ezekiel?"

"No."

"I'd recommend investing in a good six-gun in case you need to do any closeup shooting."

Ezekiel nodded.

Keeper reached for Ezekiel's rifle. He frowned at the barrel where dirt clung and rubbed it with his vest. "You leave dirt in the barrel it'll clog it and blow your damn self up. Use a rod with a cloth to clean the inside of it. And oil it after cleaning so it doesn't rust."

He continued to mutter as he dug the worst of the dirt out of the barrel then threw the gun to his shoulder. "The farthest tip on the lowest branch to my right." He sighted and fire.

The branch dropped to the ground.

"Okay, Ezekiel, you go first."

The man spread his feet as he'd seen Keeper do and sighted down the barrel.

"Call it."

"Same branch."

He fired and hit a branch three limbs up.

"Not bad." Keeper stood with his hands on his hips, his eyes squinting into the sun as he followed Ezekiel's progress. "Next time keep your focus on the front sight. Try not to flinch or close your eyes when you fire the gun."

After spending most of an hour with Ezekiel, he turned to Jacob. "Are you ready, young man?"

Jacob nodded, his eyes shining, shifting back and forth on his feet and swinging his arms in impatience.

"Let's see if you were paying attention." He handed him the rifle after opening the action so that the chamber was visible. "It's best to open the action before handing a rifle to anyone. That way you both can see if it's loaded or not. And keep your finger away from the trigger until you're ready to fire."

Jacob gave a solemn nod, pointed at a branch on his right, sighted down the gun barrel and fired.

The limb floated to the ground.

"That's some good shootin'. Boy, you're a natural." Keeper patted Jacob on the shoulder, approval in his voice.

Jacob glowed.

"You mean I did better than, Dad?" Jacob's eyes widened.

"Son, your father is probably smarter than both of us put together. They don't let just anybody practice law."

"My dad is smart," Jacob acknowledged.

Keeper let him shoot for another half hour then they headed back. He felt somewhat more comfortable leaving the women, knowing at least the boy could handle a gun. And to be fair with some more practice, Ezekiel would do fine. What he lacked in skill, he made up for in determination. If it came down to it, Maybell was no slouch with a gun either. They'd be okay.

How had he let himself get so involved in other people's lives anyhow? The Widow O'Donnell. He'd done a fine job of minding his own business until she bulleted into his life. He shook his head and muttered under his breath.

"Did you say something, Mr. Tyree?" Jacob asked from the back of the roan.

"Just reminding myself to mind my own business."

"Why?"

Before he could respond, Ezekiel answered. "People have a right to their privacy, Jacob. You should always honor that, unless they ask or need our help. Then you step in and do what you can."

"Didn't I tell you your dad was smart?" In better humor, Keeper grinned and kicked his bay into a canter.

As they reined in at the pink monstrosity as Keeper thought of it, Jacob jumped off the roan and ran inside.

"I want to thank you, Mr. Tyree."

"It's Keeper and you've got nothing to thank me for."

"We both know better. You've made sure my son can be proud of his pa. Not many men would have seen the need or done anything about it. I'll take the horses down to the stable at the other end of town." He took the reins from Keeper and nudged his horse into a trot. His back straight.

Hands on hips, Keeper stared after him then muttered, "You're not bad for a bookish sort." And then and there decided that this odd assortment that he would be riding away from tomorrow was going to be all right.

~*~

As Maybell promised, they were all treated to dinner at a place called The Green Apple. She'd made them all bathe and in spite of her sore shoulder helped haul water from the pump out back.

"We're going to get a pump in the kitchen," she told Juanita as the group trod down the sidewalk, the sounds of skirts swishing, everyone clean and in their best duds, which for him and Cathleen meant clean shirts and trousers. The women dressed as respectable as if they were going to a church picnic, their faces devoid of makeup.

The sun set in a blazing ball of glory as they entered The Green Apple, the smells of roasting beef and potatoes making Keeper's stomach growl.

As they stepped through the door, they spied one empty table and headed for it. A stringy gray-haired woman with a pruny face stepped in front of them, dressed in black and gray plaid, a white apron wrapped around her waist. "Are you the soiled doves that are taking over that pink whore house?"

Keeper's back went up. Before he could say anything, Maybell stepped forward, ready to go toe to toe. "Why, ma'am, how kind of you, most folks just call us whores."

Titters and gasps sounded from nearby tables.

Cathleen stepped forward. "Are you saying our

money is no good here?"

Before she could reply, a harassed older man, also wearing a dishcloth for an apron, hurried forward. "For God sake, Martha." He stepped in front of the frowning woman. "As long as you can pay, we're happy to service you. I apologize for my wife."

The beanpole of a woman turned and stomped away. He seated them himself then followed his wife.

"It's going to be a pleasure taking her business away from her, once folks get a taste of Juanita's cooking." She raised her voice. "Juanita's Café will be opening in a month, in the Pink Monstrosity."

Keeper smiled at the name. Maybell must have read his mind.

People stared. Most of the women with disgust. Most of the men with doubt and interest.

The proprietor came hurrying toward them with a tipper-handled, blue-flecked graniteware coffeepot. A woman in a high-collared brown cotton dress, sitting at a nearby table, reached out her hand to stop him. "James Morris! You don't intend to serve those people, do you?"

Keeper'd had enough of sanctimonious, supposedly-Christian townspeople. He started to rise then settled back in his chair when the proprietor answered. "Yes, Agatha, I do. My job is to feed people not judge them. More coffee?"

She rose with a huff, her chair scraping across the floor. "Well, if you feed them, you won't be feeding me. Come, Horace."

The plump middle-aged man rose reluctantly. He

gave an apologetic shrug and said in a loud whisper as Agatha hustled out, her nose in the air, "It'll blow over."

"Counting on it." James' expression bland, he ambled over to their table.

"Coffee?"

The adults turned their cups up. He poured then grinned at Jacob. "Milk, young man?"

"Yes, please."

"I'll have it out in a jiff. We're serving roast beef, potatoes and green beans. That work for everyo ne?" He set his pot on the table and turned to Maybell. "Did I hear correctly? You planning on opening a café at your place?"

"Sure am. Is that a concern for you?"

He waved an arm that encompassed a full room. The only open table, the one that had been recently vacated. The bell over the door rang and a cowboy stepped in. Took a quick look around and strode toward the empty table.

"It'll be like this till closing. We've got more business than we can handle. Actually, I'm looking forward to it."

"You're a good man. We appreciate your kindness." Maybell took a sip of her coffee from a sturdy, white ceramic mug, then raised it in salute. "You make an excellent cup of coffee."

"I don't judge and I expect others to do the same. Though, not everyone falls in line with my thinking, including the missus. It was she who made the coffee."

He made his way back toward the kitchen, stopping to chat and pour coffee as he went.

"You don't meet too many like him. If he wasn't already wed, I'd toss my bonnet and my garters at him." Maybell watched his progress.

"Why would you do that?" Jacob gave her a questioning stare.

"Jacob—" his father began.

"That's a real good question. Maybell, you've got money and independence, why throw that away only to tie yourself down?" Keeper reached in his blue vest pocket for a cigar then thought better of it.

Maybell gave out her hearty laugh. One that had heads turning in her direction. "Well, bless my soul, Keeper. You and I are too old and set in our ways to be put in harness, aren't we?" Her eyes gleamed.

You'd think she was poking a stuffed toad, Keeper thought half-amused, half-aggrieved.

"You don't believe in marriage, Mr. Tyree?" Cathleen inquired.

He thought they'd moved past the mister. Apparently not. "Might be fine for other people. What about you, Mrs. O'Donnell? You were married. What do you think of it?" And wasn't this the dang blamest conversation.

"I imagine with the wrong person it would be downright miserable. But with the right partner it's the most wonderful thing in the world."

As he watched her the others fell away. All he saw was her face, filled with softness, light and sadness. "I take it yours was wonderful."

"Yes. One I have no wish or hope of repeating."

Since he had no desire to marry himself, he didn't understand why his stomach churned and his heart grew heavy.

His glance traveled around the table. The women were silent. Betty Lou actually wiped at her eyes. Ezekiel looked like he'd been gut punched and Jacob just looked bewildered.

To his relief, he saw James and sour-faced Agatha making their way towards them carrying large, heavy platters. He grabbed up his fork and knife. "Here comes our food."

As the plates were set in front of them, they dug in. The aromas rising with the steam causing more than one stomach to growl. It also ended any uncomfortable conversations.

They finished off their meal with slabs of apple pie that had flaky crusts and a taste of cinnamon.

"Thanks, Maybell. That was a mighty fine meal." Keeper tossed down his white linen napkin.

"It was indeed. How about if we head back? I'll give you a good cigar and a whiskey. And anyone else that would like a drop."

"Now that sounds good to me." Keeper pushed to his feet.

Maybell left money on the table and rose. Chairs scraped as the rest of the party did as well.

They had almost made it outside when a cowboy reached out and grabbed at Juanita's fanny as she walked by. Keeper'd had enough. It had irritated him past bearing that the proprietor's self-righteous wife had been rude to the women, but Juanita was barely more than a child. One that looked ready to cry.

He grabbed the cowhand by his collar and hauled him out of his chair. "Let's take this outside," he said in a pleasant voice. A voice that would have alerted anyone that knew him. He dragged the man, trying to gurgle a response, across the floor and through the door then drew back his fist and for the second time that day knocked down a man who'd disrespected a woman.

CHAPTER 6

Rubbing his knuckles and feeling better than he had all day, Keeper stepped over the motionless cowboy.

"Gosh." Jacob breathed. "That's the second man you've knocked down today, Mr. Tyree."

Before he could respond, his father said gently but firmly, "Fighting is a last resort, Jacob."

"Yes, sir," the young boy mumbled, kicking at the sidewalk with a scuffed boot.

"But sometimes it's necessary, especially when a woman's honor is at stake."

"Yes, sir!" Jacob's head snapped up and he grinned widely.

"Your pa has the right of it, young Jacob." Keeper clapped him on the shoulder. The little boy looked up with a bad case of hero worship limning his face. "Always protect a woman's honor."

"Yes, sir," he repeated.

Their good-sized group clogged the sidewalk, their boots and shoes clattering on the wooden slats.

A small man in a wool suit, stepped to the side and let them pass. Doffing his derby, he nodded and smiled. "Evening ladies. Gents."

"I'd say my choice of El Dorado was a good one." Moonlight illumed a smug expression on Maybell's face.

Juanita remained silent.

Keeper noticed. "Don't let one no-account cowboy put you off, Miss Juanita. No matter where you go, you're going to run across men with no more sense than a rutting mule and that's a fact."

She gave a small smile. "I never thanked you for coming to my rescue, Mr. Tyree."

He looked uneasily into her upturned face that right now resembled Jacob's after Keeper had punched out the unruly cowboy.

"Don't think nothing of it." He made a dismissive gesture with his hand.

By now, they'd reached the Pink Monstrosity, it's white gingerbread trim gleaming like candy in the moonlight. Ezekiel held the door as they all trooped inside.

"There's a good bottle of scotch in the parlor if anyone has a mind and cigars for the gents."

"Thanks, Miss Maybell, but I'm going to get Jacob to bed."

"Oh, Pa." Jacob began to protest.

"Don't argue with your pa, son," Keeper said.

"Yes, sir." His head drooped in a dejected manner.

"I think I'm going to stay outside and get some fresh air." Cathleen hung back.

The rest of them trooped into a large room with overblown roses on silk wallpaper. The dustcovers piled in the corner.

Maybell opened a mahogany serving cabinet and drew out crystal glasses. She blew the dust out and poured a goodly amount of the amber beverage in each of the glasses and passed them around. "Cigars are in the drawer on the right, Keeper."

He helped himself to one, took out the cutter laying nearby and snipped off the end, then sparked a lucifer off his boot and drew on the cigar till the end glowed a bright orange.

He took a puff then a swallow of whiskey. It warmed his belly and his mood. He lifted his glass in Maybell's direction. "A good cigar, a good whiskey, good company following a good meal. What more could a man want?"

Dora sashayed up to him. "Come to my room and I'll show you, Keeper."

"Dora, behave," Maybell commanded. She wagged a finger at Dora. "You have a bad habit of giving what you can get paid for."

Dora shrugged and sashayed over to Betty Lou and begin talking about a hat she'd seen in the mercantile window they'd passed.

He knew Maybell well enough to know it had nothing to do with the coin, though she was a sharp business woman, and more the fact that for some odd reason, she considered him to be Cathleen's property.

"Keeper." Maybell moved to the door. He followed. She led him across the hall to her set of rooms and opened a small velvet purse lying on a table that still had the dust cover on it.

"I can't begin to repay you for what you've done for

us." She opened the drawstring purse.

"Then don't."

"I always pay my way."

"Your money's no good with me, Maybell."

"Wouldn't think of offering it, Keeper."

She took his hand and dropped an antique garnet ladies ring, with a delicate gold filigree edging, in it.

"What the hell, Maybell?" He stared at it. Then her meaning hit him upside the head. He pushed it back at her. "It's not happening."

"Do with it what you will, but someday you may find you have a need for it." Before he could give it back or toss it on the table, she pushed him out the door.

He shoved the ring in his vest pocket. Who'd of thought such a hard-headed business woman as Maybell would turn out to be a matchmaker at heart. Ah well, it would make a nice trinket for Molly. Or maybe give it outright to Cathleen and tell her it was a gift to her from Maybell.

And speaking of Cathleen, he'd best remind her they needed to make an early start in the morning. He strode onto the porch, lit by the full moon that had followed them from the café. A horse galloping by muffled the tinkle of the doorbell as he opened it. He stopped in midstride, Ezekiel on the porch too.

On his knees, Ezekiel captured Cathleen's hands. "I know you don't love me, but please stay. With time, I'm sure I could change your mind."

The food in his stomach coalesced into a hard ball. He backed up unseen, strode into the parlor and to everyone's surprise, picked up the scotch bottle and headed to his room.

~*~

He sat his horse, as edgy as a corralled bronco, the dawn sky streaky with grays and pinks, the streets still, except for a lone proprietor up the block unlocking his store. Tetchiness—he wouldn't call it nerves, men didn't have nerves—settled as Cathleen strode out of the Pink Monstrosity, shoving her worn Stetson on her head, the light color contrasting with that raven's wing hair. Her boots rapped across the wooden planks of the porch and then she was swinging into the saddle of her horse that he had waiting for her.

"I wasn't sure you'd be here." He reined his stallion in a half-circle and nudged him into the quiet street.

"Why?" She blinked in surprise as she trotted up beside him.

Looking neither left nor right, a scrawny black dog came running out into the street and under Cathleen's horse's nose.

Her mount half-reared.

Keeper reached out to grab the reins but she'd already brought the roan under control.

"Well?" She settled in the saddle.

"Well, what?"

"Why ever did you think I wouldn't be here?"

"I happened to step out on the veranda last night when your beau was proposing." He touched his vest pocket where the ring lay.

"You think I would let anything come between me

and taking down Pardee?" Her color heightened, her look incredulous.

"You could do worse." His voice sounded grudging, even to his own ears.

Her voice gentled. "Ezekiel is a good man."

"Can't argue that."

"You just don't think he belongs out here."

"Do you?" He turned up his collar, waiting for the sun to warm his skin and sooth his aching bones. You'd think he was fifty instead of forty-six. Came from hard living he supposed.

"Everyone deserves a second chance. His wife died. He wanted a fresh start."

"I'd say El Dorado is that all right. Let's pick up the pace. We're burning daylight." Effectively ending the conversation.

They rode hard all day and covered a goodly amount of ground. At sunset they found a grove of rough-barked, tight-budded trees blooming near a small stream, and made camp.

By the time he got the horses settled, Cathleen had a fire going and the coffee on. Their supper consisted of jerky and hardtack.

They sat on a rough log in front of the campfire, the silence comfortable, as if they'd done it a hundred times before. The flames, orange tinged with blue leaping toward the sky, warmed the chill in his bones. He pulled out his flask and held it out.

She shrugged and took it.

A grin pulled at his lips, as silver flashed in the firelight when she tipped it back. Along with an outline of a long, white throat. He didn't concentrate on that, instead teased. "Looks like I've corrupted you. What would the good ladies back in El Dorado think?" He referred to the snooty ole biddies that had turned their noses up at Maybell and her girls.

"I'm not like them."

"Never thought you were." He took back the flask and had a healthy swig.

"Not even when we first met?"

His mind flashed back to her walking through the café door. Her black dress in stark contrast to her white, brittle features. The only sign of life on it, were those fire-banked eyes, flashing so much hate and despair it'd nearly shriveled his heart.

"Mrs. O'Donnell," he began.

"I thought we had moved past the more formal names."

"Cathleen. I make it a habit to never pry into anyone's business or offer advice, but I'm going to break my rule. In this case, probably to my everlasting regret. You lost a child and I'm sorry for it, but you are lucky enough to have one left. A beautiful little girl that needs her ma."

"You've never had children, Keeper?"

"No, ma'am, I haven't." He sat down the flask. Picked up a stick and drew mindless circles in the dirt.

"My child. Born of my pain, my blood, my sinew, was murdered and the man that did it laughed while my son's breath labored and his heart stopped."

Her grief overwhelmed him, beat at him like ice pellets, making him want to get away from it. Hide from it.

Instead, he reached for her and said in an unusually gentle voice, "Cathleen."

She shook her head and held up her arms as if to ward him off.

"I seek no solace. There is none. Can be none, until that man is as cold and dead as my son. When I spit on his corpse, it will be over and I can return to my daughter as whole as I'll ever be."

"Alright. Get some rest. We'll leave at daylight." He dropped his hands and let the air whistle out of his lungs in a weary sigh.

~*~

Overnight, the temperature dropped. The sky full, the air heavy and damp. A cutting wind blew causing them to burrow into their dusters when they set out the next morning. White vapor drifted in the air whenever the horses snorted. At midday they hit the river, wide and sullen.

"What river is this?" Cathleen drew her duster, spattered with mud, tighter around her, reining in at the rocky bank. Her horse stomped and tossed its head.

"Cottonwood." He took his hat off, ran restless fingers through thinning hair, then shoved it back on. He stared at the swollen banks, the current moving fast. Water slapping at the shore. "They've had rain. This river is ready to overflow." As he spoke, fat snowflakes began to fall.

"What do we do? We can't cross."

"There's a raft we can use to cross—" He looked up and down the river. "About a mile down. At least there used to be. Unless we wait and cross tomorrow. It'll be a rough ride today." He glanced at the white flakes landing on the tips of waves, holding momentarily then disappearing.

"How far are we from the badlands?" She stared around her.

"If we keep moving, we could make the edge of it by tomorrow night."

"Let's go then. Which way?"

"Right."

They reined their horses to the right and trotted forward, ignoring the whistling winds and fast dropping snow, accumulating on the ground and red hides of the horses, as best they could.

They kept moving. Keeper constantly gazing along the river bank.

"Haven't we ridden more than a mile?" Cathleen fought back a shiver.

"Almost there. See those two trees up there?"

She shifted forward. "I don't see a landing."

"No, but there's the raft in the trees."

"I thought we were taking a ferry."

"Nope. An old boy I know keeps a raft on either side of the river. He's got a cabin on the other side. He'll put us up for the night. We can get ourselves and the horses out of the weather. Otherwise, I'd throw a tarp up between a couple of saplings and wait it out.

"There it is." He pointed. "Should be an inlet just past those trees." He nudged his horse forward, rode past the trees then jumped down. The raft bobbed on the water, tied to a rough-hewn stake at the water's edge.

Cathleen rode beside him. "Do you think it's safe?" Her expression skeptical. She quieted her horse who skittered as the raft thumped against the rocks.

Keeper tied his horse to a willow bent over the water and jumped on the raft. It rocked hard as he walked across it. He grabbed the rail as the raft rose on a rising wave then thumped down.

"It'll hold and there's room for the horses. Let's get it done before the weather gets any worse." He glanced at the gray, overloaded sky and got a face full of snow.

Unwrapping the reins, he led his horse to the raft. The bay drew back his ears and balked.

"Come on you mule this isn't the time to get nervy."

"Let me." Cathleen slid from her mount, and talking to her quietly, led her onto the raft. Nerves quivered under the horse's hide, but it obeyed. She tied the reins to a ring on the raft then came back and repeated the process with his horse.

"You've got a way with you." He admitted, shaking his head.

"Too bad it doesn't work with recalcitrant males." She tossed him a saucy smile.

Pretty sure he knew who she referred to, he kept his mouth shut.

Once the horses settled, he pointed at a loop of rope attached to the side of the raft. "Get inside that. It will keep you from slipping off the raft."

"It has a rail."

He tamped down his impatience. Urgency thrummed through him. Between those full clouds, the wind that continued to rise, and the back of his neck that pained him like a rotten tooth, he had a real bad feeling about what was coming. He fought back the edginess and looked her in the eye. "I'm hoping the weather doesn't get worse till we are across, but I'm not counting on it. The deck is going to be slick and the raft is going to heave. I don't want you going overboard." Then stunned them both. "Please."

Without a word, she slipped into it. He cataloged that surprising acquiescence and would think about it at a later date. He untied the rope holding the raft to the stake, grabbed the pole, hoisted himself into the rope loop on the opposite side from Cathleen and pushed off.

The muscles in his arms jumped and quivered as he pulled against the current. The snow blinding. It was all he could do to see the far shore. Cathleen grabbed the pole nearby and did the same. He gave an abrupt jerk of his chin in approval. He needed all the help he could get.

As they rowed, the waves got choppier and higher, splashing across his boots on a regular basis. His muscles screaming, he pushed harder.

The snow picked up. The black outline of the trees on the other side of the shore his only marker. He hoped to hell he'd gone in a straight line and didn't end up a mile up stream. He pushed on, ignoring the pain in his arms and back. Taking a moment, he wiped the wet from his eyes, scanned the horizon and frowned. Were they closer or was it his imagination? No, they were closer.

With renewed vigor, ignoring discomfort, he rowed harder. Then, as if to laugh at his moment of hope, the wind began to shriek and the waves rise. The horses began to sidle. His bay stepped on Cathleen's roan causing it to rear and try to break free.

Before he realized what she was about, Cathleen slipped out of the rope holding her in place and fought her way to the horses.

"Cathleen, get back." He motioned with his arm.

He cursed as she ignored him. To his intense relief she reached the horses without sliding into the river or getting trampled or kicked. Soon, she had them quieted. As they settled, she began slipping and sliding back across the raft.

The wind gave a howl. The raft tipped.

"Cathleen!" He scrambled out of the safety rope but knew he was too late. He watched in horror as she slid into the river.

CHAPTER 7

Fatigue jolted out of his system, blood arrowed through his veins, every sense alert. He tore off his boots, guns and duster, threw them to the middle of the raft and dove in.

He'd been shot once. The bullet lodged between his shoulder and neck, hence his arthritis. When he hit the water, the waves knifed him much the same. They tore the air from his lungs and swept pain through every damn inch of his body.

He arrowed to the surface and looked around. No sight of her. He cursed the high, gray lapping waves and the snow blurring the horizon. Drawing air deep into his lungs, he went back under. He turned in a circle.

Nothing.

Once again, he shot to the surface. Got his bearings and went back.

Nothing.

All he could see, gray water.

Again, he broke through icy waves.

Again, he went back down, his heart pounding, fear coursing through him. She couldn't drown. He wouldn't accept that. He dove deeper and continued down till his ears rang, and his head grew light.

A strand of wet silk tickled the back of his hand. He reached out and grabbed it. Just a thin water weed. If he wasn't afraid he'd drown, he'd be cursing long and loud. When another strand caressed him he ignored it. Then her face bumped against him. Cathleen! He got a grip of her hair, knifed to the surface and pushed her face above water.

"Cathleen."

No response.

He swam for the bank, pulling Cathleen with him, kicking hard with his legs and stretching out with his free arm. He had to get her to shore and get her breathing. It only took minutes but felt much longer as he hauled her up on the rocks to the wet ground, rolled her over and began pushing between her shoulder blades.

"Stop." She got out before he could push on her again. Water gushed out of her landing in a pool beside her head.

He hauled her up and pulled her against him. His hand in her wet hair, his arms wrapped around her, he shuddered, his heart thumping. "You scared me." He spoke in a low voice against her hair.

"Me too. Horses." Her teeth chattered.

"Horses? Horses!" He jumped up and squinted at the horizon. Relief surged through him. The raft had drifted to shore and now bumped against the snow-buried bank, several yards away.

Trotting, he headed toward it, his legs refusing to move any faster. He stepped on a sharp rock, cursed and kept going. He reached the raft, his breath whistling as his lungs pumped icy air in and out, working double time. Grabbing the towline, he tied it around the trunk of a tree then grabbed his boots, one of them lodged in the water between the bank and the raft, the other hanging over the side, the toe hooked on the raft, the shaft in the water. He hauled them out, emptied them and put them on.

A sleeve of his duster also dragged in the water. His guns and holster miraculously still on the raft. He retrieved his guns, put his gun belt on with stiff, cold fingers then put on his duster and led the horses off.

He squinted through the flakes, trying to get his bearings. "Well, goldang."

Straight ahead, the dark outline of a cabin broke through the driving white. For once luck broke their way. With a groan, he threw a stiff leg over the saddle and gathered Cathleen's mount's reins and headed back to where he left Cathleen.

A few minutes later, he reined in. He blinked in confusion, certain he'd left Cathleen here, beneath the old oak with a broken lower branch. He rose in the saddle, cupped his hands and called, "Cathleen."

The sound came back a muffled echo.

"Cathleen."

Straining to see through the white sky, he nudged his mount forward. His bay took half a dozen steps and stopped at a snow-covered log.

The log moved.

He jumped off his bay and drew Cathleen into his arms, hastily wiping the snow from her face.

"Cathleen!"

"Cold." Her teeth chattered.

"I don't doubt it. Just hold on another few minutes. We are almost there." He wiped the snow off as best he could, took off his duster and wrapped it around her, settled her in the saddle then climbed up behind.

"Let's go." He thumped his heels against his horse. One hand leading her mount, the other balancing her and holding his reins. The horses picked their way through snow well past their fetlocks and rising.

"Stay with me, Cathleen. We're almost there." He gathered her close, protecting her as best he could from the falling snow blanketing them, blasting cold and wet against bare skin.

Her body shook against him, reminding him of her fragility. Alabaster skin over thin bones. "Dammit, Cathleen, you hold on. You hear me?"

The horses slowed. He blinked through the snow. There! There was the cabin.

"We made it, Cathleen. We made it.

"Gooseneck." The bellow muffled by the snow.

Silence.

No fire drifted from the chimney. No hee-haw from Gooseneck's mule or bark of warning from his dog.

The saddle creaked as he climbed out of it, Cathleen in his arms. He strode up the steps onto a porch with a couple of inches of white on it. "Gooseneck," he bellowed again, as he kicked the door open and strode into an empty room.

A layer of dust coated a large cold fireplace made of river rock that Gooseneck had hauled to the cabin himself. It also lay thick on the rough-hewn table his friend had made from a nearby pine he'd cut down.

He rolled Cathleen in a musty bearskin that lay on the floor and carried her to the cot, his wet boots tracking across the dusty, wood-planked floor.

"Cathleen."

"Hmm."

"We've got to get these wet clothes off you. Can you help me?" He touched her frozen hair then pulled off his tan duster he'd draped over her.

She roused enough to say between chattering teeth. "Horses."

He shook his head. "I'll see to them as soon as I get you dry." His hands rigid with cold, he managed to pull off her boots. Dust rose when they landed with a thud on the floor. Off came the socks, revealing long slender feet that felt like ice in his hands.

He pulled off her duster, then her sodden trousers. He looked at the bloomers clinging to her slim person and decided they could stay on. Attached to a plain black garter was a leather sheath with a wicked-looking knife in it. He found that oddly titillating and left it in place.

"Whew." His breath whistled through his lips as he held her up and pulled off a wide-sleeved shirt. The wet chemise clung to high, small breasts. "We'll leave that on too." Wet himself, he was feeling plenty warm.

He wrapped the bearskin tightly around her then lay her back on the bed. Without bothering to change into dry clothes, he fought his way through fast-building drifts to the wood pile, grabbed an armload and made his way back. He threw the logs into the fireplace, added some corn cobs in a box next to the fireplace and a year-old newspaper and struck a lucifer. The flames caught, then smoked as they lapped the damp wood, then found the dry and shot up the chimney.

The fire going to his satisfaction, he pushed to his feet. The blood knifing through his veins thickened and slowed. He realized just how tired, how cold he was. His breath whished out, white in the cold room. Couldn't be helped. He had to see to the horses.

He pushed through the door. It shrieked in protest as he thumped it shut, then strode across the porch and dropped knee deep into snow. Just a few days till spring and they were in the middle of a dagblamed blizzard. He grabbed the horses and they slogged their way through the snow to the lean-to behind the house. He led them in, took off their saddles and gave them oats from the bin. The open area faced the house, so for the most part, they were protected, as long as the wind didn't change. He patted the horse closest to him, threw the saddlebags over his shoulder and trudged back, bones creaking.

Stomping his feet on the porch, he shoved open the cabin door. A blast of heat, at odds with the bitter cold, wrapped around him and weakened his knees. He leaned against the door for a moment, catching his breath, then moved to the fireplace, pulled off his boots and shucked his clothes. Something thunked and rolled across the floor.

"Well, I'll be damned." Somehow Maybell's ring had survived the wetting in the river. Picking it up, he shoved it back into his vest pocket then sank into the rocker, sticking his feet out to the flames. He grabbed the jug beside it and took a swig. Finally, his insides warmed. He leaned his head against the back of the chair, the jug dangling from his fingers.

"Keeper." The raspy voice woke him from his half doze and had him pushing to his feet.

"Cathleen." In two long strides he was beside her.

"Where are we?"

Stiff joints protested as he knelt beside her. "A friend's cabin. We're safe."

She nodded and closed her eyes.

He lay his big, callused paw on her forehead. Heat shot through his palm from her dry, hot skin. Fever.

Surprise jolted his system when she reached up and took his hand. He blinked, his breath stuck in his throat. He couldn't remember the last time a woman had held his hand, maybe not since his ma. His bent-over position awkward, he didn't let go. After a bit her grip loosened and her breathing evened. Still, he held on.

It wasn't until she tugged it loose and rolled over that he let go, pushed to his feet and strode to the rocking chair. It scraped as he yanked it across the floor, leaving lines in the dust as he pulled it up beside Cathleen's bed and dropped into it. His head resting against the tall back, he fell layers deep into exhausted sleep.

As a weak sun filtered through a dirty east window, he woke. To his shock their hands were once more entwined. He studied them bemused, hers so much smaller, almost the size of a child's by comparison.

Well, he'd better untangle them or she'd take that knife of hers to him when she woke. As gentle as possible he loosened his hand, surprised by the feeling of loss that washed over him. He shook his head. He was getting old and soft.

He tossed off his melancholia. The horses needed seeing to and his bladder was about to bust.

Dancing, glistening flakes of snow whooshed in as he opened the door. He clomped through the thick white flakes that lay like a blanket on the porch. White far as the eye could see. Dang pretty if you didn't have to be out in it.

He stepped off the porch into snow up to his knees and wondered yet again about his friend. He trusted he was holed up somewhere snug and warm, maybe with a willing widow or soiled dove. He cursed and tried not to think of the widow in the cabin and turned his thoughts to Molly, lusty and willing.

He shoved through the snow, the cold considerably cooling his wayward thoughts. After he relieved himself, he saw to the horses then went to make sure the raft hadn't come loose and floated down river.

He had to make his way along the water's edge for a bit. A quarter mile past where he left it, he found it bobbing in the snowy water, hooked up in some waterlogged tree roots. Wrestling it free, Keeper hauled it down to where Gooseneck kept it moored then tromped back toward the cabin. He was almost there when he heard a high thin scream.

CHAPTER 8

He rushed forward, stretching out his legs, fighting the thick snow, his arms pumping, his heart pounding. Gun drawn, he burst through the door. A roughly-dressed stranger, with a thick beard, grasped his arm where a knife protruded. Cathleen sat up on the cot, clutching a torn chemise. The cabin and everything in it turned red as Keeper's temper spiked. He cocked the gun in his hand.

"Keeper, don't. Just get him out of here."

Keeper gritted his teeth. His finger lingering on the trigger.

"Please."

With more will power than he knew he possessed, he holstered his pistol, reached out and shoved the knife in deeper before he pulled it out and threw it on the floor.

The would-be rapist screamed.

He grabbed him by the back of a buckskin coat, dragged him out of the cabin, raised his fist and flattened an already crooked nose. Blood spurted. The man howled again. He hauled off and hit him between the eyes and knocked him right off the porch.

"Get out of here before I kill you." He rubbed his

knuckles, his blood lust only partially cooled. The man stumbled into the snow towards a horse tied in the trees, leaving a trail of crimson droplets in the snow. As far as he was concerned, letting the man live was a mistake. Keeper knew his type. He'd continue to prey on the helpless. But he didn't want to upset Cathleen more than she already was. She'd been through enough. Nearly drowning in an icy river then being attacked by a no good, worthless—he shook off the anger and strode back in. She'd made a good accounting of herself. Her backbone pure steel.

Her shirt on, Cathleen was pulling up her pants.

"Did you kill him?"

"No." His pulse ticked in his jaw.

"Would you have?"

"If you hadn't asked me not to? In a heartbeat." His voice flat.

She nodded then went back to buttoning her pants, her hands shaking.

"Are you alright?"

"Yes." The cot groaned as she sat on it and pulled on her boots.

"I'll fix us some breakfast."

"I can do that." She stood up and headed for the pantry.

"Sit, Cathleen. I'll take care of it."

She must have been more upset than she was letting on, because she put up no argument, just dropped into the rocker, leaned her head back and closed her eyes.

He studied her. White as a sheet and rings around

her eyes that would make a raccoon proud. Her beautiful hair lacked luster. It usually shone like a raven's wing. Especially when it caught the sun.

"Don't stare."

He started. "What makes you think I'm staring?"

She didn't open her eyes. "You're drilling holes in me."

"Humph. You running a fever?"

He started to reach a hand to her forehead, but figured she'd swat it away.

"Not a serious one."

He snorted. "What's the difference?"

"The difference is I'm ready to travel."

He snorted again.

"I wish you'd stop that."

This time he rolled his eyes and headed for the pantry to see what ole Gooseneck had in the larder. The door creaked when he opened it

"Ain't going nowhere today. The snow is up to my knees. It'd be too hard on the horses."

She sighed and burrowed deeper into the chair. "You aren't just saying that are you?"

"Why would I do that?"

"Because you think I need the rest."

"You do need the rest and there's a foot of snow on the ground. If you don't believe me, hie yourself out of that chair and look outside."

"I'll take your word for it."

He shook his head. He'd never met such a cantankerous female. He couldn't figure out why he found that or her so attractive.

He stuck his head in the larder and found coffee. He knew he could count on ole Gooseneck for that. And canned peaches. He must have a lady friend. Smoked venison. Flour and oats and sugar. Pulling out Gooseneck's battered coffeepot, he stoked the fire, added water and beans to the coffeepot and hung it on the blackened iron hook in the fireplace. After the coffee stopped burbling, he poured it into a chipped ceramic cup and took it to Cathleen.

Fearing she'd fallen asleep, he placed the warm cup in her hand. She wrapped both hands around it. "I want to thank you for your many kindnesses."

"I'm just doing my job." He stepped back, his voice gruff. Thanks made him uncomfortable.

He found a blackened kettle and tossed oats and water in it then slung it over the fire where the coffeepot had been a few minutes before. He pulled the peaches out and plunked them on the table. He loved peaches. When the oatmeal was done, he poured the thick mush into bowls, added the peaches and placed them on the table. While he was rummaging through a drawer in a small rough-hewn cabinet, Cathleen asked quietly, "Why'd you never marry, Keeper?"

He jumped like a stuck toad. Got himself under control and answered, "I'm gone a good bit. A wife and kids need a man around."

"Surely, there're other jobs." She pushed herself out of the chair, trudged to the table and plopped down.

He shrugged. "I'm good at what I do. And I suppose

I never met the right woman. Eat your gruel."

She took a cautious bite then smiled. "It's good."

"No need to act so surprised."

He grinned and she grinned back. "Oh, that was no act."

He laughed and plunked down on the bench across from her and began to eat.

It was surprisingly comfortable. They were easier with each other than they had been thus far. And the coating of pain and brittle that usually cloaked her had temporarily fallen away.

When they finished, she picked up a tin bucket sitting near the hewn-out kitchen sink. "I'll melt some snow and wash the dishes."

"I'll get the snow, you rest. If it warms up today, we'll head out tomorrow." He took the bucket from her. "I've yet to meet a woman that can help herself when there's a dirty dish or sock lying on the floor."

"Lucky for you," she shot back, her sapphire eyes flashing.

"Yes, ma'am, it is." He flashed her a grin that had her jaw dropping. He swaggered out the door, for once getting the last word in. Bright sun had snow melting. White wet hit the top of his boots. He stood for a moment enjoying the warm rays of sunshine falling on his neck, soothing the constant ache of arthritis then scooped the slushy snow in a bucket and trudged back inside. He repeated the process a couple more times before making one last trip. He placed it on the floor in front of the fire and pointed at it. "I imagine you'd like to clean up. I'll be outside." He grabbed a clean shirt and threw open the door.

"Keeper."

He paused. "Yes?"

"You're not planning on cleaning up outside are you?"

"Wouldn't be the first time."

"I can't let you do that. Give me a few minutes then you can come back in and clean up yourself. I promise not to peek."

He snorted. Then added, "I thank you as does my arthritis. I'll see to the horses and give you some privacy." Again, he started out the door.

"You have arthritis?"

At this rate the horses would starve. "Scar tissue from where I took a bullet several years back. Now I better see to the horses." He strode out the door letting it bang behind him, wondering what had turned his taciturn traveling companion so chatty. A deeply private person, he didn't ask a bunch of questions, even seemingly innocent ones and in return he expected the same. But that was dealings with another man. Women were a whole different kettle of fish. Nothing was sacred. They were bewitching creatures but awfully curious. Not that sharing information on his affliction was intrusive. In fairness, he was the one who'd brought it up. He'd said it without thought, because since they'd sheltered in the cabin, he'd found her too easy to talk to and let down his guard. If he was brutally honest, telling her about the arthritis made him sound old and he was sorry the minute he'd said it. Though, he was a fool to worry about it one way or another. Truth was he was old. No point in trying to sugarcoat it.

He liked to think that for a man closer to fifty than forty he was in decent shape. Give or take the thickening of his middle and thinning of his hair. And why in tarnation should it matter anyway? He had to be getting old to even be worrying about it.

Settling it in his mind to his satisfaction, he trudged through the melting snow to the lean-to behind the house and took care of the horses. By the time he finished brushing and feeding them, he figured Cathleen had time to see to her ablations.

When he strode back in, carrying a bucket of slushy snow, she had on a clean shirt, had combed her hair and smelled of fresh air and soap. A scent he preferred over cheap perfume. She stood at the sink washing dishes.

"You're supposed to be resting."

"I'm done." She shook the water off her hands and dried them on a bleached flour bag then sank down into the rocker.

He looked her over. She'd given in way too easily. Her eyes were circled and her skin sallow. Good thing they were staying put another night.

He put the bucket down in front of the fire and peeled off his shirt, dunked it in the bucket of icy water and began to wash down. Goose bumps popped up on his skin where it came in touch with the cold cloth.

"Where'd you get that scar on your left shoulder that runs down to your ribs?"

He turned to find her staring and raised a brow. "Thought you weren't going to watch?"

"I guess I lied."

He shook his head, chewing on a smile. "Got in a fight with Bad Joe Malone. He didn't take kindly to me hauling him to jail."

"Found this in the cabinet." She tossed him a worn white towel.

Catching it with one hand, he dried off, threw it around his neck and proceeded to hunt for a mirror. He found one collecting dust in the corner of the pine cabinet that stood between the kitchen and living space of the cabin. Dampening his chin and jaw, he scraped his hunting knife across his face.

Cathleen had fallen silent. He glanced in the mirror. Her eyes were closed and her breath even. Good. She needed the rest. It would be hard come by for the rest of their journey. He was more relieved than he could say that she hadn't caught a lung infection from her time in the icy arms of the river. The woman was tough as nails. But what would happen to her when she no longer had her hate to keep her going?

The thought left a sour taste in his mouth and a knot in the pit of his stomach. He threw the towel to the floor.

Cathleen slept through the day. By the time she woke up he'd heated up some beans and coffee for supper.

She strode to the door and opened it a crack. "I've slept all day. The sun's going down." Surprise coated her voice.

"Take advantage of it. It's probably the last chance you'll have."

The door creaked as she shut it.

"Sit and have a bowl of beans." He placed two bowls on the pine table and poured coffee.

She slid onto the bench and took a sip of her coffee. "Thank you."

He nodded.

"You're a contradiction, Keeper."

"Why do you say that?" His mug halfway to his lips, he paused.

"You can be hard as nails."

"Glad we finally got on the same page about that."

She laughed. The sound rusty as if she didn't laugh very often. Which was purely a shame. With a little use it would sound like bells tinkling.

"And you can be one of the most considerate people I know, in a gruff way of course."

He snorted.

"You remind me of…" Her voice trailed off.

"You don't have to tell me if you don't want to."

"Oh, I don't mind." She took a sip of her coffee then sat it down.

"My brother."

"How so?" He scooped up his beans.

"Tough on the outside and soft as a marshmallow on the inside."

"Well now. I don't know if your brother and I have been insulted or complimented." He picked up his mug and gulped down coffee. "What's your brother do?"

"He died of influenza last year."

"You have my condolences. You've had a lot of grief for one so young."

"I'm hardly young." Her laugh brittle.

"From where I'm sitting you are."

"You aren't that much older than I am."

"Missy, those eyes aren't nearly as sharp as they appear."

She just shook her head.

To both their relief, the talk switched to generalities. The cabin darkened as the sun set and they retired. Cathleen to the cot and Keeper to the bearskin rug in front of the fireplace, his saddle his pillow.

At daybreak, they were on their horses and forging on. Their breath white in the cool air. The snow had melted to within an inch of the ground. What remained had frozen over. Snowy ice fractured beneath large hooves, crackling with each step.

As soon as they swung into the saddle, the easy comradery of the night before disappeared. The widow's composure as brittle as the bare branches that moaned in the brutal gusts. Keeper glanced from right to left as they pushed on. Tension rippled just under his skin. One of the things that kept him alive in a business that many didn't survive was an animal instinct.

The wind held a tang he could taste on his tongue. The air thick, making breathing hard. The horses nervy. Though that could be a reaction to him. He didn't know when or how but danger waited.

He kept moving, even when the sun overhead told him it was time to take a break. Cathleen never wavered. Her gaze always straight ahead, like a lode star, no doubt fixed on finding Pardee and killing him.

The snow began to melt with the heat of the sun, turning the icy crust to slush that the horses slogged through. Trees and outcroppings of rock sprang up breaking the miles of barren white. They had just passed a wide-branched oak when a shot rang out.

CHAPTER 9

"Low in the saddle, Cathleen and ride like hell. Don't stop for nothin'," he bellowed, gun already out of his holster, the other hand on the reins as he wheeled his horse around. The sun glinted off a rifle barrel on his left behind a waist-high rock.

He ducked another shot then fired in rapid succession.

A rifle slid down the rock and a man fell to the ground. Gun still drawn, Keeper nudged his mount forward. The horse sidled then settled. Keeper brought the stallion to a stop beside the shooter. Sliding off the horse, he toed the man over and cursed. It was the sidewinder that'd attacked Cathleen in the cabin. He should have killed him when he had a chance. That was twice now he'd let someone live and regretted it.

He stared at the dead man. The face partially hidden by a bushy beard. Still, it looked familiar. Of course! Walleye Wallace. He'd seen that face on a wanted poster. If he'd looked closer at the eyes, he would have recognized him. Things were looking up.

Whistling, he rounded up Wallace's horse, took Wallace's bedroll and wrapped him in it. Cathleen came galloping up as he tied Wallace onto his saddle.

"Aren't you going to bury him?" She reined in beside him.

"Weren't you supposed to keep riding?"

"What if you'd been hurt?"

"Would have been all the more reason for you to keep going." He adjusted Wallace on the saddle then mounted, leading Wallace's horse.

"Aren't you going to bury him or is the ground too hard?" she asked again.

"Taking him to Hays. There's a bounty on his head. He's worth one hundred and fifty U. S. dollars dead or alive." Having a bounty to collect definitely put him in better humor.

"We can't do that."

"Oh?"

"That will take us out of our way. Add another day or two to our journey."

"Mrs. O'Donnell, has it slipped your memory that your payment of one hundred dollars is short four hundred and expenses?" He strove to keep his voice level, but he couldn't stop his teeth from gnashing.

"No, it has not." If possible, she stiffened her poker-rod back.

"We'd be going close to or through Hays anyway. We should get there by late afternoon. Sleep in real beds, head out tomorrow morning at daybreak and enter the badlands by tomorrow evening." He mentally rubbed his hands at the thought of a bed and hot bath.

"Fine." Her teeth clicked together. Without

another word, she reined her horse, tapped her heels to the animal's flank and trotted away.

"Wrong direction, Mrs. O'Donnell." He just managed to wipe the grin off his face when she turned and glared at him. He rubbed his chest, swearing he could feel ice pellets piercing him from those eyes.

He swung into the saddle and headed west, Cathleen close behind.

They made good time and pulled into Hays as the sun lowered, undecided whether to set or not. The sky a pretty rose backdrop against the huge orange ball. The town sprawled out ahead of them. A mercantile, stable, several hotels and saloons visible, with a church steeple in the distance.

He pointed at the closest hotel, a two-story building with a coat of gleaming white paint. "Why don't you get us rooms and I'll hunt up the jail."

"I don't have any money." Color lit up her cheeks.

"I'll pay for the rooms when I get there."

"Add it to my bill." Her chin notched up, her color still running high.

"Oh, I will." His mood still good, thinking of the bounty.

He found the jail without any trouble, left Wallace and collected his bounty. He headed back to the hotel to make sure Cathleen was alright. When he found the rooms had been booked without incident, he headed to the saloon.

The doors swung backward as he strode in to noisy comradery and the yeasty scent of beer. He stepped up to the bar.

"Beer." Pictures of scantily dressed ladies flanked a large mirror behind the bar. The bartender poured him a foamy draft and shot it down the shiny wood counter. He caught it in his left hand, downed half the mug, wiped his mouth and thumped the beer on the counter. The tension between his shoulder blades easing.

A brassy blonde wearing a bright red dress with a fitted bust and flared skirt that rustled when she walked sashayed up to him. "Buy me a drink, handsome?"

"Well, I don't know about the handsome, but I never turn down the opportunity to have a drink with a pretty lady," he said with a gallant sweep of his hat.

"Hey, gramps." The call came from a skinny young man leaning on the bar at the other end, a shiny six-gun at his hip, hot eagerness in his eyes, twenty at the outside.

"Ignore him, honey. He's looking for trouble."

"Yeah." He turned his back on the youngster with the fancy gun belt and silver-banded black cowboy hat.

"Hey, gramps."

Keeper sipped his beer.

"Aren't you Keeper Tyree?"

Chatter died away and the dozen or so patrons sitting at round tables or leaning against the bar turned to look at him.

"That's right, youngster."

"Youngster?" The young man straightened. The man in between them stepped away, leaving his drink on the bar. "Are you calling me a kid?"

"Figured that out, did you?"

"I'm going to have to insist you apologize."

"I just came in for a beer, son. I'm not looking for trouble." He'd seen the type too many times to count. Young and eager to make a name for themselves. Add another notch to their belt. Thinking no more of gunning down a man than they would a rabbit. Perhaps, less.

"Well, you've found it, gramps."

"Just walk away," the blonde said in a low voice.

"Wish I could. But I've seen his kind before. One way or another, he's going to be pulling that gun and I don't fancy a bullet in the back. Best you step back."

Reluctantly, she did so.

He turned slowly and his gaze drilled into hot brown eyes. "Are you in that big a hurry to die?"

The kid's gaze faltered then returned to cocky. "I'm not going to be dying today." He stepped away from the bar and stood with legs spread, shaking his fingers, his hand resting a few inches from his gun.

Keeper never dropped his gaze from the young gun's, analyzing, assessing, and knew the exact moment the youngster made his decision.

As the kid went for his pistol, Keeper drew in one smooth motion and fired. Normally, he aimed for the heart, taking no chances of a shot in the back, but he couldn't help thinking of the needless death of Cathleen's son.

The kid's hand flew to his shoulder, blood dripping through his fingers.

Keeper gave him a long look, holstered his gun and went back to his beer.

"Look out!" Someone called out.

He whirled. The boy had grabbed his shoulder with one hand and pulled his pistol with the other.

Keeper fired.

The young gun crumpled, blood spurting from his chest, his gaze now sightless.

Keeper shook his head and plunked down a couple double eagles. "Somebody see he gets a decent burial."

The bartender nodded.

He turned and strode out, his shoulders shoved forward with each stride, his heels clicking, anger and sorrow in his heart. He hoped to hell Cathleen did not find out about this. She would not take it well. Couldn't say he blamed her.

Mounting his horse, he rode back to the hotel and signed the register with a bold, large scrawl.

"Nice to meet you, Mr. Tyree. I don't get to see many famous folks. If you need anything just let me know." The innkeeper, a large hearty woman, winked at him. "Though, I've met your traveling companion. Still and all, my offer stands."

He tipped his hat. Traveling with Cathleen was bound to set the gossip mongers talking. Couldn't be helped.

The bell jangled as he strode outside, took the horses and rode a few blocks till he reached the local livery and stabled the horses. From there he headed to the nearest barbershop, with his saddlebag over his shoulder. He noticed Cathleen had taken hers as well.

Hopefully, they had a bathing room at the hotel.

He found a barbershop with a bath attached. Had a shave and a bath and came away feeling better except for the hole in his stomach. It was past eating time.

He strode to the hotel, trotted up the stairs and rapped his knuckles against the door.

"Just a minute." The door groaned as Cathleen opened it wearing clean trousers and a deep-blue shirt, her hair wet and on her shoulders.

"You hungry?" He rocked on his heels.

"There's a hole in my belly you could walk through."

"Then let's go plug it up." He made a gallant gesture with his hand.

"Just a minute let me put up my hair."

He wished she'd leave it down, but knew enough to keep his mouth shut. She left the door open. He stepped inside and watched her twist it in a bun and stick pins in it. He looked around while she grabbed her hat. Plain white walls, a brass bed with a green duvet and a picture of the mountains on the far wall. A blue and black wool rug covered a good portion of the floor. Nothing fancy but plenty good enough and clean. He hoped his room looked as good.

"I'm ready." She adjusted her hat. "Are you taking your saddlebags?"

"Forgot I had 'em. I'll drop 'em off. Looks like I'm next door."

"Yes."

"Did the innkeeper give you a bad time?" He remembered the ribald wink.

"Nothing I couldn't handle. I was surprised they gave me a room without me paying for it, but your name did the trick. I guess I didn't realize how well known you are."

He shrugged it off. "Shall we go?"

She nodded, came through the door and shut it. He threw his saddlebag into a room similar to hers except the wool carpet had a few more cigar burns in it.

Their heels clicked as they set a good pace down shiny oak stairs that someone's boots had left a clump of dirt on. They headed for the hotel's restaurant and stopped in the doorway. Tables covered with white cloths were packed with customers chowing down. Silverware chinked against china. A harried waiter rushed by. Keeper reached out and slowed him with a hand on his arm. "How long a wait?"

"Mister, I've got no idea."

He dropped his hand and the man hurried on.

"There's a café across the street. Want to give it a whirl?"

"Sure." She threw one wistful glance at the restaurant then turned around.

"We can eat here." He'd caught the look.

"It looks nice. Clean, well kept, a quiet crowd. But if I have to wait much longer, I may grab a steak right off the next plate going by."

"Then let's try that café. I wouldn't want you strung up for rustling beef." A laugh rollicked out from deep in his belly.

She joined in. The sound less rusty than it had been in the past. It made him think of angels and heaven. He mentally cursed himself for his fanciful thoughts. It wasn't like him.

They headed out the door and stepped into the road to cross the street, where lights from the café and a couple of saloons lit the area along with a thousand stars and a big ole Kansas moon. A horse came charging through the dirt, his rider whooping. Keeper grabbed Cathleen and pulled her out of the way. He pressed her to his side and stood clenching and unclenching his free hand, of a mind to go teach the cowboy better manners.

"Lots of action in Hays. Let's go eat." As if she knew the suppressed anger that rode him.

"Yeah." He became aware of warmth and smooth muscles beneath his hand, savored it for a moment then let go.

They hustled across the street. Scents of fried beef, fresh coffee and spices greeted them as they pushed through the door. Spit pooled in his mouth and he heard Cathleen's stomach gurgle. He scanned the tables and nearly swore. This place was full up too, mainly cowboys.

"There," Cathleen pointed at two men in black trousers and black jackets that pushed back their chairs and rose from a nearby table. As the men headed toward the door, a matronly-looking waitress saw them standing in the doorway and motioned them to the table. She picked up dishes as Keeper pulled out a chair for Cathleen then plunked himself down.

"The special and coffee?" She balanced two cups

on top of dirty plates.

"Ma'am, if that wonderful beef I smell is your special load it up." His voice boomed and he beamed at her.

"Coming up." She gave him a smile and hurried away, gray skirt rustling.

"You do have a certain rough charm."

"Why thank you. I think."

The waitress returned a moment later with two steaming cups of coffee then hurried back to the kitchen.

"Think we'll make it to the badlands tomorrow?"

"We should, barring no complications. From there, no tellin. The badlands have a thousand hidey holes. All kinds of places he can disappear in." He noticed concern in her eyes. "We'll find him. I'm just letting you know it may take awhile."

"Oh yes, we'll find him." Her expression hardened and her jaw tightened.

The waitress hurried back with steaks that still sizzled and set large white no frill plates down in front of them.

"If those steaks are as good as this coffee we are in for a real treat."

Her eyes lighted and she blushed, livening her worn features. "I made the coffee."

"Never had a better cup." He toasted her with it.

"I'll bring you a refill."

"That would be grand."

She hurried away.

"That was kind of you."

He forced himself not to squirm and answered in his gravelly voice, "Just spoke the truth."

"Kind," she repeated, eyeing him over her white ceramic coffee cup.

"For someone that's hungry you don't seem in a big hurry to eat." He cut a large bite from the steak and forked it in.

She followed suit. Conversation ceased till they finished. He leaned back in his chair tipping it on two legs. "All that's missing now is a cigar and a good glass of whiskey."

"Well, I can't help you with the whiskey but be my guest with the cigar. Everyone else is." She fanned the air.

"I'll wait." He took note of the waving hand and flashed a grin.

A drunken cowboy came weaving by and bumped into their table. He tipped a brown cowboy hat. "Sorry, ma'am." He then tipped his hat in Keeper's direction. "Say you're Keeper Tyree."

"That's right." The rasp in his voice more pronounced.

"I was in the saloon this afternoon when you shot that mouthy kid. Can't think of anyone who deserved it more." He wove away through the tables.

That tears it. Eyes that had warmed to violet returned to artic blue, chilling his heart and reminding him of how those eyes looked when they first met.

"What did he mean when he said you shot that mouthy kid?"

"Just what he said." He threw down his napkin. Never apologize. Never explain. It was rules he lived by.

"I see." Even her voice iced over.

"I doubt it. Let's go." He shoved back his chair and tossed some bills on the table.

She pushed past him and headed toward the door. He stayed on her heels as she hurried outside, making no attempt to walk beside her. Knowing she didn't want him there. A drunken cowboy reached for her as they bulleted across the street and stepped onto the sidewalk in front of the hotel.

"I wouldn't." Keeper stepped in front of Cathleen.

The cowboy took one look at Keeper's face and backed up into a horse trough where he fell in, water arcing all around him.

The two ignored him and entered the hotel.

Cathleen swept up the stairs with Keeper trotting after her. Silently, they made their way to their rooms neither speaking to the other.

Keeper unlocked his door and banged it shut behind him. He grabbed a flask from his saddlebag, dropped on the bed and pulled off his boots. The fine steak he'd wolfed down sat like a rock in his gullet. He took a long swig from the flask and let the rotgut loosen his belly. For the life of him he couldn't figure out why her reaction bothered him. He didn't give a good damn what people thought of him. Couldn't figure out why he cared now.

He drained the flask and fell asleep on the bed with his clothes on.

Hammers pounding in his head woke him as dawn stole into the room. Dang, he was going to have to stop drinking. The hangover offset any enjoyment rotgut temporarily brought. Why had he anyway?

Memory surged and a picture of icy blue, accusing eyes rose in his mind. He couldn't really blame her. She'd lost a son to a fast gun. Wouldn't leave one too rational about hearing about another kid dying young. Well, nothing he could do about it. She'd get over it in her own time or she wouldn't.

The bed groaned as he pushed to his feet, threw water on his face and followed the smell of coffee downstairs, his boots clicking loud as thunder on the shiny wooden steps.

"Good morning." A suited gent nodded as he made his way up the stairs. Keeper winced as the voice banged around in his brain.

He strode to the hotel's restaurant, dropped down in his chair and managed not to grab the coffee out of the waitress's hand when she set it on the table. He hoisted the heavy white mug and downed the contents. The hot liquid rolling down his throat in a tidal wave of pleasure before he plunked the mug back down. "I'd be obliged if you hit me again."

"Eggs and bacon?"

"Just toast."

"Coming right up." She poured the fresh dark brew into his cup then hustled into the kitchen.

A shadow fell over his table. He looked into Cathleen's expressionless face.

"Mind if I join you?"

He didn't answer, just rose and pulled back her chair. He had no inclination to converse with anyone this morning.

The young lady with a sweet smile and a white apron tied around her green dress, hurried back at sight of Cathleen. She carried a cup and the coffeepot, poured Cathleen coffee, refilled his cup again, took Cathleen's order and left.

A local paper had been left behind on the empty table next to them. He grabbed it then disappeared behind it, occasionally reaching around for his coffee. He was beginning to feel like he'd live. Maybe he should have ordered bacon and eggs after all. He caught the waitress's eye. She hurried over, smiling.

"I'll have some bacon and eggs as well."

"I'll get that order right in."

"Thankee kindly."

She flashed her pretty smile and hurried to the next customers that had just sat down. Keeper disappeared behind his newspaper.

Cathleen cleared her throat.

The headache that had disappeared came thundering back. He lowered the paper reluctantly and waited. Her words took him by surprise.

"I owe you an apology." His eyebrows rose but he said nothing.

"The young man you killed left you no choice."

"How did you come by that knowledge?"

"The maid and Matilda."

"Matilda?"

"Matilda. The innkeeper. Everyone's all atwitter

about it. Haven't you noticed the way that young waitress keeps looking at you? You've become larger than life."

"Not sure killing a man is any reason to become famous."

"I believe it's got something to do with the number." Her voice dry.

"And what number might that be?"

"The chambermaid said fifty. By the time I talked to Matilda it had went up to sixty."

"Good God." His eyebrows shot up.

"Numbers not right?" Her eyes while not the warm violet he occasionally caught a glimpse of were no longer icy enough to give him frostbite.

"Not hardly."

"What would be the correct number?"

"Don't you think that's a bit salacious? I've never notched a man's life on my gun belt. And I've never killed anyone that didn't deserve it." And that was as close to an explanation as he intended to go.

Before he could raise his paper, their breakfast arrived and they both dug in.

An hour later, they were in the saddle and headed for the badlands. They rode steadily through the day. They arrived at the badlands late in the afternoon. The sun, a glowing circle of fire, hit the large sandstone boulders, the sky red in the background.

They reined in.

"It's quite beautiful," Cathleen said.

"It is that." He stiffened.

"What?"

"Riders."

She followed his gaze. "Oh, my God. What are they doing to that man?"

"Dragging him." His raspy voice grim. It wasn't an easy way to die.

"We've got to help him."

"Unless someone is harming a woman or child, I don't interfere in another man's business."

She threw him an impatient look, thumped her heels against her mount's sides and shot forward, straight toward the four vigilantes.

"Cathleen. Wait. Dammit to hell." He flapped his hat against his stallion's shoulder and the horse took off, churning up bits of sand and dirt beneath his hooves.

"Stay back," he yelled as he passed Cathleen, brought his horse to a stiff-legged halt in front of the men, tied the reins around the pommel and drew both guns.

The hombres plunged to a stop in front of him.

"What the hell. This Injun a friend of yours, mister?" The bewhiskered man dragging the body and sitting a pinto, asked.

"No friend of mine."

"Then I suggest you mind your own business."

"Normally I do."

"This is no concern of yours."

"Agreed."

"Then move."

"Can't do that."

The man on his left put his hand on his pistol.

"I wouldn't." Keeper pointed one gun at him.

Cathleen came riding up and reined in alongside him. His spine tightened. Things just kept getting better and better.

"Get back." He didn't look at her. Didn't take his eyes off the four men. For a wonder she obeyed, backing her horse up. She had her duster on and her hat low on her head. If they got real lucky, the hombres would take her for a boy. Luckily, they were more interested in him at this point.

Keeper motioned toward the man on the ground. "Leave him and you live."

"Mister, there's four of us."

"I can count."

"You won't be so cocky when you're lying in a pool of blood." The man with small eyes and pockmarks on his face, drew his gun. Keeper fired then shifted and fired again. The two men crumpled and fell to the ground. The man on his left drew his gun. Keeper fired. The man on his right, took off in a cloud of dust.

Keeper swung out of the saddle. Three men lay on the ground. Two dead. The man in the center had fallen straight down. Keeper toed him over.

He groaned and looked at Keeper from eyes already glazing over. Blood turning the chest of his shirt crimson. "Who are you?" he gasped.

"Keeper Tyree."

"Just my luck." His head fell to the side and his breathing stopped.

Keeper checked the other two men.

Cathleen came riding up in a cloud of dust, threw

herself off the horse and ran to the bound man and knelt beside him. "He's alive!"

"No bounty here."

"Is that all you can think about?" she snapped.

"Well now, considering I'm going after Pardee the next thing to pro bono, it does weigh on my mind."

"I can help you find Pardee."

CHAPTER 10

The voice had Keeper jerking around. Surprise turned to anticipation. He reached the Indian in three long-legged strides.

Calm brown eyes stared into his. The man had taken a beating no doubt about it. He'd been dragged over stones and rough terrain and had the bruises and missing patches of skin to prove it.

In one swift move, Cathleen drew her knife from its holster. It gleamed sharp and deadly in the setting sun.

The man's eyes lost their tranquility. Unease shone through.

With swift sure movements, she began to slice through the rope.

"You know Pardee?" Keeper asked.

"Yes."

"How?"

"I spend a good deal of time in the badlands." His answer evasive.

By now the ropes had been cut. The man sat up then cautiously rose to his feet, wincing.

Keeper studied him hard. "Ain't seen you on no wanted posters."

"Good to know." The man flashed him a white-toothed smile.

He had long black hair, now tangled with weeds, high cheek bones, a nose smaller than Keeper's that looked like it had managed to stay unbroken. Keeper had a vague mistrust of men that managed to keep their nose in one piece, though this one did have a scar below his right eye an inch or so long that told him the feller had seen more than one fight in his lifetime.

"One of your parents white? You speak mighty good English."

"Keeper!" Cathleen gave him a scandalized look.

"What?" Women. Wonderful creatures but you never knew what would set them off.

The man laughed, winced and touched a cut lip. "My daddy was school teacher to the Kickapoo tribe."

Well, that should put him right up there with the lawyer in Cathleen's book. For just a moment, Keeper regretted his lack of education.

"Sam Brown." Sam held out his hand.

Keeper took it. Sam's grip firm. The hand callused. He liked that in a man.

"Keeper Tyree."

"I've heard of you." The man's grin fell away.

"Most have," Keeper said in his gritty voice.

"I'm twice over relieved that I'm not on a wanted poster."

"Lucky for you, you're not.

"This is Cathleen O'Donnell." He gestured in Cathleen's direction.

He took her hand and bowed over it. "Ma'am."

"Mr. Brown."

"Sam please. I owe you both my life."

"You owe her not me. I make it a habit not to interfere in another man's business. She was the one that went riding to the rescue. If I'd been alone, you'd still be kissing sagebrush."

"You may have been an unwilling participant but it doesn't change the fact that I'm in your debt."

"You find us Pardee and you can consider my half of the debt paid."

"Mine as well." Cathleen spoke up.

"I'll find you Pardee."

The sun that had been in a downward spiral hit the horizon, blazing off the sandstone, burning crimson and turning the sky a perfect blend of pink and purple.

"We won't be going much further today. Let's aim for that large boulder to break camp. It'll cover our backs." Keeper pointed at the pinto. "Want to take that hombre's horse? He looks like a good one."

"He's my horse and he is a good one." He whistled. The pinto trotted over, snorted and laid his head on Sam's shoulder. Sam gave him a pat.

"Your horse seems to like you. That's good enough for me." Keeper rocked on his heels, his hands in his pockets, laughter behind his eyes.

"Yes. If the ladies liked me half as well, I'd be the most popular gent in the Western states."

Man had a sense of humor. Keeper liked that too. He flashed a grin then sobered. "Let's mount up."

"Let me see to Mr. Brown's wounds first." Cathleen

protested. Blood dripped steadily down his right arm, coating his hand and dripping off his fingertips.

"Why I thank you, ma'am, and it's Sam. But Mr. Tyree here is right. Being at the base of the badlands without protection's not a good idea."

They rode for another mile, while the sky lost its pink and turned to a bluish grey accented by several eager stars fighting to make their appearance. In the distance a wolf howled. A lonely sound when Keeper rode alone. Tonight, it just blended with the prairie.

He held up a hand to halt them when they got to the large boulder. Another tall stone bumped against it. They'd be protected on two sides if needs be.

Sam nodded his approval. "I'll start a fire."

"Let Cathleen see to you or she'll fret. I'll start the fire and take care of the horses."

He hobbled the horses then built a fire. Cathleen tended Sam. While the fire jumped into the sky in bright orange flames, crackling and snapping, the embers shooting for the heavens, Keeper made coffee in his old battered pot and hung it over the fire then dug out their meager supplies.

They sat leaning against the boulders and ate jerky and hardtack.

"Do you have kin left, Sam?" Cathleen sipped her coffee.

"My parents passed and I don't have any siblings. My dad had a heart attack. My mom went shortly after. I swear she died of a broken heart."

"They must have loved each other very much."

"Yes, ma'am, they did."

"Where did they meet, if it's not too presumptuous for me to ask?"

"They met on the Kickapoo reservation where my dad taught any folks that were willing to learn. In exchange they taught him to speak Algonquian."

"Did you have a happy childhood, Sam?"

"One of the best. Some people might consider me an outcast, but my pa and ma made sure I knew my worth."

Keeper cut in. "How far are we from Pardee?"

"Maybe a day. Maybe a few days."

"I didn't think the Badlands were that large," Cathleen said, obviously chafing at any delay.

"You're right. But it's comprised of chalk hills that rise a hundred feet over the Smoky Hills River. And everything in between twists and turns. It's like riding through a maze. Pardee has several hidey holes."

"You're a Godsend, Sam."

"Well, I don't know about that, ma'am, but I'll do everything I can to help you out. By the way, we gotta keep an eye out for wild buckwheat. It isn't good for the horses and it flourishes around here."

"Again, you're a Godsend and please call me Cathleen."

He nodded and flashed her a smile that lit his eyes in the firelight. "Cathleen."

"Where we headed?" Squatted in front of the campfire, Keeper picked up a branch laying on the ground and tapped it against the ground in an absent gesture, making an indention in the sand and dust.

"The cantina."

"A cantina? In the Badlands?" Keeper's eyebrows shot up.

"Not much more than a shack and tucked away where it's not easily found. The badlands and bad men have their secrets."

"I'm guessing you've got some of your own."

"That a problem for you?" Sam's friendly features hardened, revealing a stranger that could be dangerous if he chose.

"Like I said. I mind my business and expect other to do the same."

In an instant the dangerous look disappeared, replaced by the easygoing man with a long scratch on his face and a purpling bruise on his cheek. But Keeper had seen the man that lurked below the easygoing exterior. Still and all, it was the dangerous side that would help keep them alive.

"Ma'am, Cathleen, I suggest when we get there, you stay close. Keep your hat pulled low, your hair tucked up and your duster buttoned up. If anyone figured out you were a woman..." His voice trailed off.

This is exactly why he hadn't wanted her to come. It took everything in Keeper to keep his mouth shut on the subject. Somehow, he managed, though he couldn't help scowling at her.

She scowled right back.

And just like that, his mad was gone. His lips twitched as he pushed to his feet. "Better get some shuteye. We'll be heading out early. Given our location, I'll stand watch."

"Wake me and I'll take the next." Sam tossed his

blanket up against his saddle, stretched it out and lay down. Closing his eyes, he pulled his hat down, which had somehow survived the dragging though it looked pretty battered.

"I'll take the watch after that." Cathleen's chin came out as if daring him to argue.

"You heard her, Sam."

A look of mollified surprise crossed her features before she too lay down.

The engorged moon drifted in and out of gray clouds, the wolf that had howled before continued his lonely song with others joining in. A screech owl hooted nearby. Keeper cursed under his breath as he jumped. Cathleen smiled and rolled over.

Near midnight he woke Sam then settled down in his bedroll.

He'd swear he'd barely closed his peepers when a lightening sky pushed at his eyelids and a hand on his shoulder had him bolting upright, his fist drawn.

"Do you beat up everyone who wakes you?" Cathleen took a hasty step backward.

"Better to tell me loud and clear to wake up than sneak up and touch me."

"I'll remember that."

He pushed up and scrubbed his face with a callused palm. "Sam." His voice gritty with sleep, Keeper woke his traveling companion then strode into the underbrush to relieve himself.

As he returned, the scent of fresh coffee wafted toward him, tantalizing and teasing as a beautiful woman. Cathleen handed him a cup as he approached.

He took a long swallow. His system took the jolt of caffeine and righted. "Good coffee." He toasted her with the cup.

"That does seem to be your standard line." The words accompanied by a smile had his lips twitching.

"In this case it happens to be true."

Twigs crackled as Sam strode out of the underbrush from a different direction. The rising sun illumed a colorful array of bruises on his cheek.

Cathleen handed him coffee.

"Thank you."

She nodded then passed out jerky and hardtack.

They ate quickly, mounted their horses and rode deeper into the badlands. Gray and brown chalk formations surrounding them. When the sun hit just right it blinded. They wound their way through narrow arroyos then started upward. The Cottonwood River twinkled below like a curving ribbon, sparkling in sunshine, narrowing the higher they rose.

The trail, if you could call it that, also narrowed. Sam's pinto's back hoof slid off the edge causing stones to go crashing below. The horse panicked when his hoof met air and let out a terrified whinny. Sam slid from the saddle and calmed it. "Best walk them till the trail widens."

His shoulders twitching, his eyes narrowed, Keeper watched Cathleen dismount on the narrow trail. Only after she was on the ground and leading her horse forward did he relax. Thank goodness for her affinity with animals.

He looked around uneasily. He hoped to the devil he hadn't misread Sam Brown. If he wanted them dead this would be a great place to do it. He looked down then wished he hadn't as yawning emptiness met his gaze until it linked up with the river. He swung out of the saddle. Dirt crumbled beneath his boot, again lodging pebbles into nothingness.

"Keeper." Fear laced Cathleen's voice.

"I'm fine. Don't fret. It'll make the horses nervy." Keeping his voice low, he said, "Sam, you better know another way down when we head back or I'll take it amiss."

Sam chuckled, the path already widening beneath his boot heels. Then under Cathleen's. Then Keeper's. Keeper's breath whistled out of his lungs. Not much scared him. He'd seen too much. Done too much. Still, all in all, he wasn't fond of heights.

"Cathleen, you all right?" She'd been awfully quiet. Probably concentrating on putting one foot in front of the other.

"I'm fine."

It took him a moment to realize they were heading downward. "Where in tarnation are we going?"

"We're almost there."

The sun straight overhead beat on his shoulders. Even though the air held a chill, and the wind knifed at visible skin, sweat beaded his brow and trickled down the back of his shirt. They mounted their horses and slipped and slid downward. Then they were back on solid ground.

"You sure there was no other way to reach that

cantina?" Keeper pulled up alongside Sam.

Ahead a small clearing opened, with a natural rocky wall on three sides. The only way in—the trail they'd just traversed. Two dilapidated wooden buildings in need of painting backed up against rock, almost as though the spot had been carved out of the sandstone. Three horses stood at a hitching rail.

The saddle creaked as Keeper leaned forward in the saddle. "Two buildings. I'm assuming one's the cantina. What's the other?"

"A trading post of sorts."

"Huh. Well let's get to it."

Cathleen fastened her duster and pulled down her hat.

Keeper swung out of the saddle. The others followed suit.

The door squeaked as Keeper pushed it open. He looked around, his eyes adjusting to the gloom. A middle-aged, unshaven man with thin stringy hair and wearing a dirty shirt stood behind the bar.

Three men sat at a round table playing poker. Unfortunately, none of them Pardee.

They strode to the bar. "Three whiskeys."

The barkeep looked them over then pointed at Sam and spit on the floor. "I don't serve his kind."

"And what kind would that be." Keeper's raspy voice even, his eyes narrowed.

"I don't serve no Injun."

"Something wrong with his money?" He turned to Sam. "You got money?"

"I do."

"Don't matter. I ain't serving him. My place I can serve who I choose."

"So, you saying his money's not good here?"

"That's right."

"Sam, your money's no good here," Keeper said in a conversational voice.

"Bigotry isn't limited to the law abiding."

"Huh. You got a point there." Keeper swung around, his tough features hardening. "Mister, he's riding with me. My money not good either?"

"I'll serve you but the Injun's going to have to wait outside."

With a swift movement for one of his bulk Keeper reached over and grabbed the bartender by the collar, hauling him halfway over the dirty bar. "You'll serve us both or I'll come around and do it myself."

He heard a scrape from the table behind him before he heard, Cathleen's, "Look out!" He dropped the bartender, whirled and fired. The man at the back table ducked as his hat went flying. "Next one will be between your ears."

"Who the hell are you?" The barkeep rasped out, rubbing his throat.

"Keeper Tyree."

Chairs scraped as the men at the table hurried out the door, leaving their poker chips behind.

"You sure know how to clear a room," Cathleen said.

"Hmm."

"I thought you didn't get involved." Sam tossed back the whiskey put in front of him in a dirty glass by the scowling barkeeper.

"Didn't know you then. I'm riding with you now." He turned to Cathleen. "Well, if you aren't going to partake." He picked up her glass and downed it.

"You too good to drink my whiskey, boy?" The belligerent bartender had moved just out of Keeper's reach.

"Don't start, barman. He's with me too."

"He's got a mighty high voice for a man."

"Boy more like," Keeper clarified, hoping that took care of the matter. Had the three men noticed? How could they not? She had a voice like a warm blanket on a cold night.

"Well, that accounts for it. But its time he learned to drink his whiskey."

"Maybe, but it's not your concern."

"My bar. My rules." The man, much smaller than Keeper puffed up like a bantam rooster.

"Well for God—"

"You want another drink." His chin notched in the air, the bartender turned his back square to Keeper and faced Sam.

"Don't mind if I do." Sam winked at Keeper.

"What's in the store next door?" Keeper hardly a fanatic about his surroundings, wiped his hands on his pants. He hoped Cathleen didn't whip off her bandana and start cleaning. This place must be driving her crazy.

"What do you need?"

"Oats for the horses, flour, coffee."

"What do you have to trade?"

"My money no good there either?"

"My store. My rules."

"You own the store too?"

"That's right."

"Just my luck. What do you have against money?"

"Really, mister? What am I going to do with it here?"

The little man—one of the most irritating, Keeper could remember crossing paths with—did have a point.

"I'll clean this place for you." Cathleen lowered her voice an octave.

"We don't have that kind of time." Keeper grunted.

The bartender gave her a look of interest and rubbed his bewhiskered chin. "Done."

"We don't have time for any cleaning."

"You got something to trade then?"

"Fine. Get it done." Keeper threw his hands in the air.

"I'll help you. It will go faster." Sam volunteered.

"You planning on taking up a broom too?" The bartender cackled as he looked at Keeper.

"Not hardly. Show these two where the cleaning supplies are then open your store."

"Cleaning supplies? What would I do with cleaning supplies?"

Cathleen blinked then rallied. "Got a broom and a rag?"

"Of course, why didn't you say so? In the back. Also got a mop and bucket."

"Could have fooled me." She kept her voice

brusque and low while she stared pointedly at the floor.

"My bar. My floor."

"Old timer, your speech is limited."

"Who you calling old. That fizz of yours don't look any too young."

"Won't argue that. Now how about we get those supplies."

The bartender stepped out from behind the bar, wiping his hands on his dirty apron. "This way." With bow-legged strides, he hiked toward a side door that connected the two buildings. It opened with a shriek that thrummed straight through Keeper, making his innards feel like a too tight string from a fiddle.

"Ever thought of oiling that door?"

"My—"

"Door," Keeper finished in resignation.

He walked into a room even dimmer than the saloon. "How am I supposed to see anything?"

"Hold it up to the sunlight." He pointed at a grimy window.

"Sunlight? No sun is getting through that window."

"I can see just fine. Must be those old eyes of yours."

"Now you're worried about my eyesight?" His irritation with the bristly, gruff-speaking bartender was quickly giving way to humor. Not that the irritation had vanished, but it had tempered a bit.

"So, you're the famous Keeper Tyree?"

"I'm Tyree."

"Well, your tall as a t yree." He cackled at his humor.

Keeper frowned down at the smaller man, but the man took no notice.

"Now what did you want? Oats and flour in sacks that will fit in saddlebags?"

"That's right. How about cartridges, coffee and beans?"

"How are you going to pay for it?"

Keeper's eyebrows rose. "My two companions are cleaning your saloon now."

"The deal was to clean for flour and oats."

"I suppose you want this—" He searched for a word that encompassed the shelves of who knew what, thrown together in no order, dirty, unpainted walls and floors that dust rose with each step.

"Store is the word you are looking for. I'll throw in cartridges, coffee and beans for this room being cleaned as well and a double eagle."

"And a double eagle?" His eyebrows shot up again and he pushed his hat down on his forehead then raised it up a couple of times. He got in the man's face, studying him closely.

"What are you doing?" The little man took a step back.

"Don't recall seeing your face on any wanted poster but you're a thief for sure."

The little man cackled and slapped his knee. "Good one. I might even throw in an extra box of cartridges for you."

Keeper grunted.

"Oh, by the way. Nobody believes that woman is a boy. Except maybe you with your failing eyesight." He snorted and slapped his leg again.

"Don't know what you're talking about." Keeper's muscles tightened and his shoulder blades twitched.

"Of course, ya don't."

Ignoring him, Keeper walked over and tried to look out the grimy window on the right. He stared at two mules and a wagon. He frowned and turned around. "Where do you get your supplies? Ain't no way those mules and wagon could get up and down that trail we came in on."

"None of your business is where I get 'em." He puffed up.

"Kinda touchy ain't ya?" He clicked his fingers. "Better throw in a bottle of your best rotgut. How much are ya going to bleed me for that?" Resignation sounded in his voice.

"Plenty." He cackled again.

They continued to poke at each other until Cathleen and Sam came through the door. Cathleen grimaced and wrinkled her nose as she looked around.

The barkeep nudged Keeper in the ribs and said in a loud whisper, "A boy wouldn't care about a little dirt."

Cathleen heard and threw him a startled look.

The barkeep winked at her.

Keeper frowned.

Cathleen turned to Keeper. "We're done."

"Afraid not."

"What?"

"I had to strike a new deal. Robber here wants this room cleaned too in exchange for the grub and bullets."

"Robber?" The bartender cackled and slapped his leg again. "You can call me Obadiah. Obadiah Jones."

"Well, Obadiah, let me load these supplies in the saddlebags then I'll buy you a drink, if my money's good."

"It's not."

Keeper raised an eyebrow.

"I'll buy you one." Obadiah cackled. His heels thumping and kicking up dirt as he walked, he disappeared through the door leading into the bar.

"Well, you've gotten pretty chummy," Cathleen observed.

Keeper wiped a smudge of dirt off her cheek with his thumb. "He grows on you. And he knows you're a woman."

She threw him a startled look. "How'd he figure that out?"

Anyone that took the time to look would figure it out, Keeper thought. Gentleness coated the steel in her spine. Her skin, always so white, had taken on a honey-color and no boy had lips that looked so kissable. But all he said, "When you hollered your warning. Thanks for that."

Before she could respond he stepped back and headed for the barroom.

"He grows on you like a tumor," a disgruntled Sam threw at his back.

"I won't argue that."

Obadiah stood behind the bar and looked around him a look of pride on his face. "I got the best end of this deal. Why I can even see myself in the counter." He rubbed his elbow on the shiny bar.

"It does look different and that's a fact."

Obadiah poured two drinks and sat one in front of Keeper.

"You gonna tell me where you get your supplies?" Keeper saluted him with it and downed it in one gulp then thumped it on the bar.

Instead of answering, Obadiah asked, "Who you looking for? A bounty hunter don't come to my door or find my door if he's not on the scent of someone."

"Pardee." Keeper's gritty voice grew gruffer.

"Know where he's at?"

"No, but he does." He motioned through the door toward Sam.

"Then I guess you'll be finding Pardee soon enough."

CHAPTER 11

Keeper swayed in the saddle as they climbed the sandstone pillars then headed back down. The sun turning boulders from gray to gold. They'd be able to get in a couple of hours before nightfall. Here at least horses could ride two by two. Riding next to Cathleen, he nudged his horse with his heels and trotted up to Sam. "Obadiah, said if we were heading after Pardee, I'd find out where he got his supplies. What did he mean by that?"

"He gets his supplies from the Caverns."

"Never heard of it."

"It's a well-kept secret. Anyone lets the word out, they die."

"Ain't you worried?" Keeper fell back to avoid a tumbleweed then reined back beside Sam.

Sam shrugged. "Everybody's got to die. The trick is to do it like a man and to have no regrets. You and Cathleen saved my life. If I didn't help you, I'd have regrets." Sam went up several degrees in Keeper's estimation. The philosophy similar to his own.

"He's so big on trading what does he have to trade?"

"Obadiah's from the Carolinas. He's got a still out

back and trades moonshine for supplies with Jonas Wilkes. Everybody's happy."

Under his broad brimmed hat, Keeper's eyes narrowed. "Thought you and Obadiah didn't know each other."

"We don't. But everyone who's traveled the badlands knows of Obadiah. Most cantankerous coot around. I wonder what it says that you two hit it off— after you taught him some manners."

"You trying to say I'm a cantankerous coot too?" Sam grinned.

"Can't argue with that." Keeper's lips turned up then he sobered. "Tell me about the Caverns."

"It's something you'll have to see for yourself."

Keeper shifted in his saddle, displeased with the vague response. "You're saying Pardee won't be alone."

"Not hardly."

"How much company can I expect?"

"Anywhere from twenty to a hundred."

"Twenty to a hundred?" Both his eyebrows and his voice rose. He'd been hoping to get the drop on Pardee when he was alone.

"The population shifts. Men come when things get too hot."

"How do you know about this place?" Keeper gave him a suspicious look.

"When you retire from your chosen profession, I'll share my story. Until then—I don't think so."

"I've never seen you on a wanted poster."

"I'd like to keep it that way."

"Why were those men dragging you?"

"Cheating at cards."

"Were you?" Keeper's voice went flat and his expression cold. He had no respect for a card cheat.

"They thought so."

"Were you?"

"And if I were?"

"If you were, I won't be saving you again."

Sam just laughed. "I've got a near perfect memory. I can remember every card played in front of me."

"Remind me not to play poker with you." Keeper's stiff posture relaxed. They lapsed into companionable silence.

Over the next couple of hours they made good time.

"Look." Cathleen, who now rode beside Sam, rose in her saddle and pointed, a wide smile on her face. Up ahead a thin ribbon of water caught the western rays and gleamed.

"Good eye." He nodded at her.

At the smell of water, the horses broke into a gallop, and kept up the pace till they halted at the stream's edge. The water rippled against the bank and sparkled in the sun.

"Let's make camp."

Keeper swung out of the saddle and scooped up a handful of cold clear liquid and drank it. Then he wet his bandana and wiped off his neck and face. Sam did the same.

Cathleen dropped her horse's reins, letting it drink, and moved a bit away from them. Rolling up her sleeves, she scrubbed every available piece of skin.

He grinned. She was no doubt ridding herself of the grime of Obadiah's.

A slithering motion heading toward her caught his eyes at the same time he heard the rattle. His body chilled.

Hearing the noise, Cathleen turned and froze.

He whipped his gun from his holster, sighted and fired.

Cathleen covered her mouth, a small squawk escaping as the rattlesnake's head went flying.

Sam strode over and picked up the five-foot long body and held it out. "Supper."

"I hope you're planning on cooking it." Cathleen shuddered.

"You all right?" Keeper asked.

"Much better than I might have been. Thank you." She gave him a shaky smile.

He nodded. "I'll make the fire."

"I'll take care of the horses and make coffee."

"I can do that too. Why don't you take advantage of that water and get yourself cleaned up? Just stay within hollering distance."

This time the smile she threw him contained more warmth. Not enough to light her eyes for more than a moment but enough to send his ole heart thumping.

"Do you think that's wise?" Still holding the snake, Sam watched Cathleen stride away.

"I'm going to trail along."

Sam narrowed his eyes.

"And keep my back turned."

"Better let her know what you're doing."

"I will. I have no desire to be called a peeping Tom."

"I'll take care of the rest then."

Keeper saluted and strode after Cathleen. "Cathleen."

"Yes?" She whipped around.

"I'm going with you."

"You most certainly are not." Hands on her hips, her eyes sparked a deep purple.

For a moment, he just sunk into all that fire and fury and had a very ungentlemanly thought before getting himself under control. Still, he was uncomfortable with his wayward thoughts and fumbled his words. "You needn't worry about me spying on you. I'll have my back to you."

"You told me to stay within hollering distance."

"That hasn't changed." He flashed her a smile.

She gave him a suspicious look.

"Do you trust me to see to your welfare?"

"Of course."

"Then you can trust me with your privacy too." He thrummed his fingers on his thighs. "Some of those men back in the cantina looked familiar, but they disappeared before I got a good look."

"And you think they'd come looking for you. Why?"

"I know it's hard to believe but I've made my share of enemies." His hands in his pockets, he rocked on his heels.

"Hard to believe indeed." She gave a brief grin.

"Whoever takes me down will have bragging rights of being a fast gun for a long time to come. Not to mention, they heard you call out for me and know I'm traveling with a woman."

"Fine. Just make sure you don't turn around unless I call out."

"You got yourself a deal."

He held out his hand to shake on it. She hesitated then put her small one into his big paw. He clasped it and was stunned at how right it felt. Such a small thing really. He didn't know why it rocked him down to his toes. They stared at one another for a long minute till finally she blinked and withdrew her hand.

He cleared his throat and motioned at a nearby oak. "I'll be right over there."

She nodded and he strode away.

Splashing sounds reached him.

"You can turn around."

He turned, slowly, wary of a trap.

Her duster, gun belt, hat and boots lay on a nearby rock. The rest of her clothes remained on her.

"I figured my clothes were as dirty as I was." She laughed and flung her arms back and forth in the clear water. She'd found a spot that came to her waist and had dunked herself in it thoroughly. She stood up, ringing out her hair.

If she thought wearing clothes hid anything, she was sadly mistaken. Her shirt and trousers clung to her like a second skin and clothed a damn fine body. A little on the scrawny side, but perfectly formed.

She came splashing out and shivered in the cool evening air.

"Let's go before you catch cold. If Sam hasn't

already, I'll make a fire for you to dry by."

She put on her boots and they strode back to camp and even though she was shivering, she seemed in better spirits. A good clean up would do that, Keeper supposed, fondly remembering warm baths, with a whiskey and good cigar. Ah well. When he got back to Dodge it would be soon enough.

Sam not only had a fire going, he'd fixed coffee and was cooking the snake. Cathleen moved up next to the crackling flames and held out her arms. She looked at the sizzling reptile and grimaced. "I'll get the hardtack."

"Stay by the fire. I'll get it." Keeper started toward the horses then whirled around. "You seen to the horses?"

"Yes." Sam looked up from his cooking.

"You're pretty handy to have around." He flashed a grin and trailed back to the stream, washed up then got the biscuits.

Tin plates, with snake and biscuits, were passed around as they sat around the fire. Crackling orange embers shot upward in an indigo sky filled with thousands of stars that burned bright as the dancing flames.

The men chomped down on the snake steaks. Cathleen grimaced and nibbled at hers. Keeper and Sam exchanged a grin. Keeper added a dollop of whiskey to his and Sam's coffee. He raised the flask. "Cathleen?"

"No. You two shouldn't be drinking either."

"Now, missy, there's something you should know.

No woman or man tells me how much I can or can't drink. But in this case, I agree with you. Wouldn't do to be impaired while on the trail, especially this trail. But a drop in my coffee at night…been having it since I was a youngster. Keeps the chill at bay."

He toasted her, took a deep gulp then tossed the rest into the flames, turning them blue and hissing.

"You still taking first watch?" Sam asked, standing.

"Yeah."

"Wake me when it's my watch."

"Will do."

"And, Sam, you wake me." Cathleen shook out her blanket and lay down.

"I will, Miss Cathleen."

Keeper shifted on a hard rock as the other two settled into their bedrolls. With a rifle over his lap, he rolled a cigarette, dragged on it and watched the moon travel in and out of gray wisps of clouds. Several hours later he woke Sam, tossed down his bedroll and fell immediately asleep.

"Keeper, wake up." A soft voice beckoned, a warm hand shook his shoulder.

His eyes closed, his body ready, he reached and rolled her under him. "Want another tumble, Molly?"

"Get off me." The sharp crack across his cheek had his eyes flying open.

"Oh my Gad." He rolled off Cathleen.

Smothered chortles were coming from Sam.

"Shut up," Keeper said irritably.

"There're riders out there," Cathleen whispered.

In a smooth fluid movement, he was on his feet, gun drawn. "Get behind the boulder. You too, Sam."

The fire had burned itself out. Bent low, Sam and Cathleen bulleted behind the boulder. In the shadows, Keeper stood his ground, his back to the tall stone, both guns drawn.

A hoof stomped. A twig snapped. Low voices carried on clear air.

"We could shoot 'em now and be done with it then figure out who takes credit for bringing down Tyree."

"No. I heard a woman in that cantina and I want her. She had a voice like honey, even when yelling out a warning. I haven't had anything but calico queens in a long time. Can't wait to try something different, even if she does wear trousers."

One of his companions snickered. "You better plan on sharing."

Burning rage arrowed through Keeper's gut then settled to icy anger. The kind that left a cool head and a steady hand. He cocked back the hammer on both guns. "Come on in, boys."

"What the hell?" One of them called.

The intruders started firing, bullets flying.

The moon that had floated in and out of clouds, drifted out, lighting the clearing and giving Keeper clean shots at three men. He fired with his right then with his left. Two men fell from the saddle. The third took one look at his fallen compadres and galloped his horse away as fast as it would go. Keeper raised his right hand. The moon drifted back behind a cloud.

"Damn." He didn't want to take a chance on

shooting the horse. He lowered his gun hand still swearing, listening to the sound of hooves galloping into the night, growing more distant till they disappeared altogether. Whirling on a worn boot heel, he called out, "Are you two alright?"

They strode from around the boulder, Cathleen held Sam's arm. "I'm alright, but Sam needs attention." Blood streamed down the side of his face.

Keeper leaped forward. Sam motioned him off. "Just a bit of flying rock." Then yelled, throwing Cathleen to the ground, "Look out."

One of the hombres on the ground was trying to rise, gun in hand.

Keeper took quick aim and shot. This time the man lay where he fell.

He turned back to his traveling companions. Both picking themselves up from the ground.

"Thanks," both Keeper and Cathleen said at the same time.

Keeper grabbed a shirt out of his saddlebag and tossed it to Cathleen. "Use this."

"Sit down, Sam." Cathleen tugged him down to a large rock, ripped the sleeve out of Keeper's faded blue shirt and began to dab at his head. "Hold this in place," she told Sam as the gash continued to bleed.

He did as he was told. She pulled her knife out of her boot and cut strips from the shirt. She rolled one into a pad then tied it on his head with a blue strip.

She stood back and studied him. "You'll do."

"Thank you."

"You're welcome."

"It's a couple of hours till dawn. Why don't you get some sleep?" Keeper was too wound up and edgy to sleep.

"It's still my watch." Cathleen folded up what was left of his shirt.

"I'm awake. I'll take it. Besides I need to see to the bodies."

They climbed back into their bedrolls and he went to check the dead men. He studied them in the streaky moonlight. The Wiley boys. He'd seen both of them on wanted posters. Damned if he could remember how much they were worth. Must be getting old. Well, he had no intention of carting around rotting corpses. He went through their pockets looking for personal items that could prove their identity.

In one pocket he found an engraved pocket watch with Bill Wiley on the cover and a couple of gold eagles. He shoved both deep into his vest pocket.

The brother had his initials burned into his rifle stock.

That should do it. He toed the bodies into the underbrush. The horses had taken off for parts unknown. Too bad. They could have used a pack horse.

It was also too bad that he'd let one get away. If he was heading back to the hideout, not only might Pardee be alerted, but every mother's son in the bunch would be looking for Keeper. He'd made plenty of enemies over the years of men on the wrong side of the law. Well, it couldn't be helped.

The boulders surrounding them had held the heat

from the sun for a few hours after it went down, but now nothing but cold poured off the sandstone. Grunting, when his stiff muscles locked up, he stretched then gathered twigs and branches and built up the fire. Her eyes closed Cathleen scooted toward it and sighed, her shoulders relaxing. The woman never complained, tough as they came in that department. It was another thing he'd come to admire in her.

She might think she was going to kill Pardee, but he'd decided to bring him in alive. She could watch him swing without having the stain of murder on her soul. He'd be damned twice over before he let someone with such purity of heart, garner a dark blemish that couldn't be removed.

He gazed at the stars. The sky an indigo blue an hour ago now held a grayish hue. Dawn would soon follow. He took the old dented tinned-iron coffeepot to the stream and filled it with water. Always alert. Always aware of his surroundings.

With a few long strides, he arrived in camp, added beans to the coffeepot and hung it over the flames on a makeshift pole. He poured a cup and hunkered down in front of the fire.

Cathleen threw back her blankets, yawned and stretched. "Do I smell coffee?"

He swore his joints creaked as he pushed to his feet. Pouring a cup, he took it to her.

"Thank you." She took a healthy gulp. Her eyes sparked. The sleep in them gone. "Good coffee." She flashed a grin that weakened Keeper's knees. He was in trouble and knew it. The sooner this stint was over, the better.

"I bet you tell that to all the men who make you coffee."

She laughed. The sound rusty, but sweet. "Besides Henry and my dad, you're the first."

"What about your husband?"

She wore a smile, a faraway look on her face, as if she'd left him and strolled back in time. "Jason was a wonderful man. But he couldn't boil water without burning it."

"Coffee making is overrated." He took a healthy gulp from his cup.

She burst out laughing. "Don't let any of the many women you compliment on their coffee hear that."

"I expect you to keep my secret." He raised his cup to her and grinned.

"It's safe with me."

Flirting on the horizon, the sun rose turning sandstone to gold and causing the stream to sparkle.

"Pretty morning." He rocked on his heels. He loved this time of day. Everything was clean and fresh with no evil touching it.

"It is."

"Is that coffee?" Sam pushed up, stretched and helped himself to the empty cup by the fire.

"Since we're all up, we might as well head out. Help yourself to hardtack and jerky."

Twenty minutes later, they were on their horses and on their way.

Sam, who'd been riding ahead, reined in and pointed. "Tracks. By the time we get to the hideout, could be a welcoming committee."

"Been thinking the same thing." He stood in his stirrups then settled back in, his eyes on the horizon. "How much further?" They were sitting ducks winding through towering boulders in the badlands.

"A couple three hours."

"Given those tracks, I think we better wait till dark and travel then. Got any suggestions where we can hole up? It's too open out here for my liking."

Sam looked around. "About an hour ahead there's an overhang we can wait under."

Keeper gave a jerk of his chin. "Let's do it."

They trotted forward, hugging the rocks wherever possible. Keeper, with reins in one hand, a rifle in the other. The butt resting against his thigh.

To Keeper's mind, it was a long hour. Half of it spent looking over his shoulder, half of it wondering if someone would be waiting at their designated point of safety. When they arrived at the overhang, he breathed a notable sigh of relief, the twitch between his shoulder blades lessening as Sam led them behind the mounds of rock to a grove of trees. Small, but large enough to hide three horses.

"You picked a good location, Sam." His joints creaking, he dismounted, put his hands on his back and stretched.

Sam jumped off his horse and strode to Cathleen's horse to help her dismount.

"Thanks, Sam. But I don't need help."

He stepped back and Cathleen threw her leg over the saddle and hopped down.

The men exchanged a glance and Keeper shrugged.

"There's a small stream, that if it hasn't dried up, you should be able to freshen up in," Sam said.

"Thanks. I'll take the horses." Cathleen gathered the reins of their mounts and disappeared through the trees.

The men watched her go.

"Kind of tetchy, idn't she?" Sam stared at the space Cathleen and the horses disappeared into.

"You could say that." Keeper watched until she disappeared from view, unwilling to let her of his sight.

"Do you trust me?"

"What the hell kind of question is that?"

"Do you?" Sam asked.

"I don't trust nobody." His voice rough, Keeper moved forward.

"That's going to make what I'm about to suggest difficult then."

"Let's hear it."

"I leave you and Cathleen here, ride in and see if Pardee is at the Caverns. If he is, I come back and get you. If not, we go hunting elsewhere."

Keeper stopped and rubbed his chin, his whiskers making a raspy sound.

"Or I could go with you and leave Cathleen here. Truth be told I'd just as soon her not go into that bed of cutthroats."

"Truth be told, I'd rather her not either. We could both go in or I could ride ahead and meet you at the entrance at dark. If he's there, we both go in and take him."

"You seem hell bent on riding ahead alone. I wonder why that is?" Keeper's jaw stiffened and his eyes narrowed.

Sam gave him look for look. "You and Cathleen saved my life. I'm trying to return the favor."

Keeper gave him a hard stare. Finally, he said, "Alright, we'll do it your way. But know this. You double cross me, I'll find you. There's nowhere you can run that I can't get to you and when I do I'll cut out your gullet and feed it to the buzzards."

"And they say Indians are bloodthirsty." Sam shook his head and gave a mournful smile.

Keeper snorted. He rocked on his heels. "You going to explain it to Cathleen?"

"Not me." Sam gave a decisive shake of his head.

"It was your idea."

"It was just a suggestion. You're the ramrod of the operation."

"Well for God—" Keeper tossed his hands in the air and stomped after Cathleen.

CHAPTER 12

"You are not leaving me behind."

Keeper had wheedled, bribed and even cursed, finally he resorted to threats. "You aren't going. If I have to hobble you right along with your horse, I'll do it."

"I'll fire you."

"Fine. Fire me. But I'm still going and you're still staying. If Pardee is there, we'll bring him back, trussed like a turkey for your Thanksgiving dinner."

They'd been arguing for hours, Sam long gone. Keeper's patience, not his strong suit, frayed as a rope about to snap.

"You'll bring him back alive? So, I can stick my knife in his black heart?"

"I'll bring him back alive."

"Alright."

"Alright, what?" His gaze narrowed, suspicion rode his spine. Cathleen never gave in easily, not that he'd call the last couple of hours easy. Hell, she never gave in period.

"You'll wait here?"

"Yes."

"Your word?"

"Yes."

He thrummed his fingers on his thighs, trying to sniff out the lie. But Cathleen didn't lie.

"Alright." He gave an abrupt jerk of chin, down then up. He held out his hand. She took it, looking him square in the eye. Her own cool blue and unblinking.

"Well, we got a good hour till sundown, let's see about hiding you and your horse."

"We're already hidden."

"Hiding you better."

She rolled her eyes.

"I don't like leaving you." The words were out before he could stop them.

She gave him a speaking look.

"But I'd like you riding into that den of thieves and murderers even less."

"Fine. I wait."

"I trust you, Cathleen."

Something flickered in her eyes but was quickly shuttered. "Let's find a spot for my horse."

She picked up the reins and walked deeper into the grove. About twenty feet in, they found a tight grouping of pine, with barely enough room for her mount. The long-needled leaves on gnarly limbs threw shadows that would keep them well hidden. She led the horse inside, her shoulder scraping against a tree, her heels grinding in cones and needles that added a scent of spice and clean to the air.

Keeper stepped back. She wasn't invisible, but someone would have to look real hard to find her. At night it would be pretty near impossible.

"You've got a good eye. That's a good spot. Get some rest. I'll be leaving in about an hour. Remember no fire."

She nodded, sat down in the thick needles on the ground, leaned back against a tree and pulled her hat over her eyes.

An hour later, he touched her on the shoulder. "It's time."

The sun had dropped and the sky had turned a murky grey. Stars were coming out but the moon remained hidden.

"Stay in your current location. We'll be back. Hopefully, before dawn."

She gave a sharp nod of her chin.

He longed to drag her up against him and kiss her senseless. Instead, he grabbed the reins of his horse and led him out of the grove. Once out in the open, he threw himself into the saddle and rode toward the caverns. Sam had told him how to reach the hideout. He'd be waiting for him on the outskirts.

Keeper rode over an hour, keeping an eye out for Sam. He reined in and listened. His horse snorted. He quieted it and strained to hear. *Clop.* Then it came again. *Clip. Clop.*

Pulling deeper into the shadows, he pulled his gun and waited.

The rider came into view. The moon took that moment to drift out from a fat dark cloud it traveled behind and shine full on the face of the rider.

His gut twisted and he swore long and low, finishing with, "That's far enough, Cathleen."

She reined in, waiting.

He rode out and halted his horse beside her. The air between them chill, swirling with tension. Finally, he said, "Where I come from, a man's word is his bond. I don't trust many and I don't trust easy. And when that trust is broken, I don't give second chances. You promised me you'd wait."

The moon lit the rise of color in her cheeks. She lifted her chin. "I didn't say how long."

"Your word, Mrs. O'Donnell. You gave me your word. I won't make the mistake of believing you again."

He touched his heels to his horse's flanks. The stallion broke into a trot. He meant it. He didn't give his word lightly and he expected the same of others. He had no time for folks that didn't do the same. Even pretty widows.

They rode in stony silence. The tension between them thickening like a brewing storm on the horizon.

Keeper straightened, alert, dangerous.

"Move deeper into the shadows. Cling to the side of the canyon," he said in a low voice. For once she didn't argue but did as she was told. His hair might be thinning and his waist thickening, but his hearing was as sharp as a hawk's.

A horse stopped a few feet in front of them. A sure sign he knew they were there. Keeper pulled his gun. "State your business, mister."

"Keeper, is that you?" Sam rode forward.

Keeper holstered his gun and moved out of the shadows. Cathleen nudged her mount and followed.

"I thought she was staying behind."

"There's been a change of plans." Keeper's voice dry.

Sam rubbed his chin. "It's going to be difficult enough getting two of us in. And if we're caught—" He looked at Keeper. "They'll just shoot us." His gaze arrowed to Cathleen. "You'll just wish you were dead... ma'am."

"You've both made your point." Cathleen's voice came out quiet and controlled though her face had whitened.

"Is he in there, Sam?" Keeper lifted in the saddle then settled back down.

"Yeah, he is. It'd be best if we wait till after midnight to ride in. Things will be quieted down a bit."

Keeper looked at the wall of sandstone on both sides. "Got any thoughts on where?"

"There's a break in the rocks a little ways back. We can wait there."

"You're awfully familiar with this trail."

"I've been on it more than once."

He didn't elaborate and Keeper didn't ask him to.

They turned the horses and rode a quarter mile or so, before Sam halted, reined his horse to the right and disappeared.

"Damn." Keeper swore softly.

"You coming?" Sam's voice echoed back hollowly.

"If I can figure where you are."

Sam chuckled. Keeper followed the sound, riding slowly as close to the sandstone as he could get without his leg scraping against it. He saw the fissure. A narrow opening, with the sandstone just a few degrees darker than the rest. It was barely higher than his head and narrow enough the horses had to go single file.

He went a few yards and the fissure widened into a small cul-de-sac composed of sandstone and trees.

"Anybody else know about this?" Keeper looked around. Sam was proving worth his weight in gold.

"Couldn't say."

"This will do just fine." He threw his leg over the saddle and climbed to the ground. Sam and Cathleen did the same.

"I think I'll get some shut eye. Sam, wake me in a few hours will you?"

Sam nodded.

Keeper gave his horse some oats, but didn't remove the saddle. He pulled his duster around him, his hat over his face and fell asleep. He'd learned long ago to take sleep where he could get it when he was on the trail.

"Keeper." Sam shook his shoulder.

He came instantly awake. "What time is it?"

"Midnight."

"You should have woke me."

"You can take first watch if we make it out of here."

"Cathleen?"

"I'm right here."

He'd been hoping she'd be asleep and they could ride out without her.

"You ready?" He looked at Sam.

"Yup."

"You ready?" Keeper walked to Cathleen.

"Yes." She grabbed her reins.

"Here let me help you."

"Not neces—"

He put a hand on her shoulder, pulled back the other, fisted it. And hesitated. He'd never hit a woman in his life.

Sam shoved him aside and clipped Cathleen on the jaw.

Cathleen crumpled to the ground. Her horse sidled, snorting.

Keeper shot Sam a look then bent down checked her pulse and stretched her out in a more comfortable position.

"What? You weren't going to do it."

Keeper straightened. "I would have done it. Still and all, glad I didn't have to. Let's go."

He swung into his saddle and they headed out the crevice and back into the canyon.

"She's going to kill us right along with Pardee," Sam said conversationally.

"Yup."

"Maybe we should have just tied her up."

"Maybe. But if someone or a wild animal was to find her—" His voice trailed off.

They rode in silence. The only sound, hooves on dirt and the occasional ring of horseshoes on stone.

"How much farther?" Keeper asked. By his calculations it was about one in the morning.

Sam reined in and pointed. Ahead lay what

appeared to be a cavern in the huge expanse of rock. Sam rode inside, Keeper followed.

When they entered the cave, Keeper looked around in amazement.

Little surprised him anymore. But this sure did. What looked like a plain cave opening on the outside spread into a huge, carved out area on the inside. Large enough to house men and horses. Torches were lit on both sides of the entrance. On the right was a paddock that held about twenty horses. On the left an entryway that led deeper into the cave.

Sam dropped off his horse and Keeper did the same, every sense alert. A couple of the horses in the paddock snorted. Shadows from the lighted torches danced along the wall. They tied their horses to a nearby post beside the corral and strode quickly toward the entryway.

Once inside Keeper stumbled as he looked around. His breath caught. It was like a city built into the stone. There were about twenty rooms on the first floor and stairs carved into stone that led to the second.

"Well, I'll be damned," he breathed.

"If anyone catches us that's the God's truth." Sam's voice barely a whisper.

Keeper tugged up his collar and pulled down his hat as they walked. Most of the entrances dark, except for a light up ahead. "What's up there?"

"It's a saloon of sorts. Late night card game going on. Just keep walking."

Keeper's muscles tightened as they crept through

the shadows and past the saloon where lights flickered, bottles chinked and voices murmured.

"How long's this place been here?"

"Few hundred years maybe."

"An ancient civilization?"

"A long dead one."

"How long have outlaws known about it?"

"Awhile."

"So, where's Pardee?" Keeper's hand slid to his gun.

Sam pointed at a darkened hole on the right ahead of them.

"How'd you find him?"

"It's like a boarding house. Pardee pays for this room year-round." He paused outside the entryway. "You ready?"

Keeper pulled his gun and leapt into the dark opening, right into a soft body coming out.

CHAPTER 13

A squawk escaped before he could clamp his hand over her mouth. The cave walls swallowing the sound. How the hell had Cathleen gotten here was his first thought. But the frightened eyes staring into his belonged to a stranger. A lantern lay on a bedside table throwing a shadowy light on Pardee sprawled on the bed, snoring. The reek of whiskey strong in the carved out stone room. The air cavern-cool.

The girl he held trembled, her skin like ice. The lamplight shone on her face. He was stunned at how young she appeared.

"We aren't going to hurt you. We are here for Pardee. Will you be quiet if I take my hand away?"

She nodded. Her eyes huge.

While Keeper untangled himself, Sam ran lightly to the bed and tapped Pardee's head with his gun barrel. The snoring stopped.

Keeper let the girl go, cuffed Pardee, while Sam pushed a dirty handkerchief in the outlaw's mouth.

"Let's go." Keeper tossed the outlaw over his shoulder.

"Take me with you." The girl's voice came out of the dark.

Keeper paused.

"Please." She begged. "Please."

Shadows from the lamp fell across the rough-hewn wall and kept her face in shadow. She moved out of the dark, revealing a cut lip and bruised cheek. Her breath coming quick and fast. Keeper's fists tightened. "Come on then. Sam, see if the coast is clear."

Sam gave a clipped nod of approval and slid through the door. A moment later, he waved a hand. Keeper motioned the girl ahead. Her back against the wall, she slunk out the entryway. He followed on her heels.

None of the rooms had doors, just cave openings.

Up ahead, voices drifted from the card game and light washed outward from the rough-hewn chamber. Sam reached the edge of it and stopped, holding up his hand. Dust spurted under their heels as Keeper and the girl ground to a quick halt.

Pardee started to stir. Keeper swung around. Pardee's head thumped against the rough rock wall and the outlaw subsided.

Sam strode along the rocky hallway passing in front of the lit entryway. Once past, he motioned for the girl. She hurried forward.

"Hey, honey. Hold up. I'm nearly done with my cards."

She froze in place, color leaching from her face.

Sam made a beckoning motion.

She hurried forward.

"Girl, did you hear me?" the cardplayer bellowed.

"She's with me," Keeper called out.

"Who is that?"

"Pardee."

"Pardee?"

"That's right."

"Your voice sounds rough."

"It was the rotgut I was drinking."

"Yeah, you were at that." Several guffaws came from the card room.

"Send that girl here when you're done."

"Will do, but don't look for her anytime soon."

More raucous laughter broke out.

Apprehension rode the girl's face in the torchlight.

Sam motioned to the other side of the entryway. Keeper gave a jerk of chin in acknowledgement, hoping for more cover. His system tensed for danger. It was narrow, just a few feet wide, but maybe it would make the difference. He pulled his hat down, strode to the other side and hugged the wall, every moment expecting a shout or gunshot.

One long stride. Two then three. Pleased surprise rushed through his system and air left his lungs in a whoosh when he was no longer in the light.

They strode rapidly through the entryway, past the dark entrances and to the corral.

"Grab a couple of horses for the girl and Pardee and get them saddled," Keeper commanded.

Sam didn't hesitate. Tack hung from the wall, where hooks had been hammered into rock. Sam grabbed two bridles and bridled a piebald and a roan. The girl seized two saddles. Gave one to Sam and tossed one over the roan. By now the horses had started milling around.

Keeper managed to undo the gate and hold on to Pardee. The gate creaked alarmingly. "That tears it. Let's go." Sam brought him the piebald and Keeper swiftly tied Pardee on. "Go on," he told the girl. "We'll catch up."

"Sam, scatter the horses." Keeper untied their horses and hopped in the saddle. "Get on," he shouted.

Sam shooed the last of the horses out of the corral.

"Heeya," yelled Keeper, riding in the middle of the panicked herd, the piebald's reins tied around the saddle horn, forcing the horse alongside his.

Sam leaped on his horse and did the same.

They'd just cleared the entrance when shots rang out.

"Stay down." Keeper rode low in the saddle as the sounds of horseshoes rang out against stone and thudded in dirt, throwing up clods and dust. The warning unnecessary, Sam rode low on the side of his saddle nearly invisible with the horses churning around him.

"Get those horses before they get away. And kill those sidewinders that stole them." The voice echoed through the caverns and carried on the cool night air.

Keeper, holding onto Pardee, turned and fired over the horses' heads. Someone cried out. More lead flew, hot and heavy. The horses, already panicked, raced faster. Harder. He hoped to hell the girl was up ahead and out of the line of fire.

A sharp jolt of pain bit into his right arm. His gun dangled from his fingers. His jaw clenched. No way was he losing his gun. Putting the reins between his teeth, he took the gun in his left hand and shoved it into his holster.

He rode low in the saddle, distancing himself from hot lead.

As they raced on, gunfire became more sporadic. Finally, it grew muffled and eventually stopped all together. The racing horses slowed. Keeper pushed his mount and Pardee's forward through the herd keeping them at a fast pace. Sam did the same.

As the stampeding horses dropped away, Keeper spied the girl. Relief coursed through him.

Sam pulled alongside. "Up ahead is where we left Cathleen."

"Let's collect her and keep going. They're eventually going to round up those horses and then there will be hell to pay." As if in response to his words, the moon that had been sporadic at best drifted behind the cloud. The path lit only by dim stars.

"You keep going. I'll gather, Cathleen."

"It might be best," Keeper agreed.

"Go straight for two miles. We should catch up by then."

Keeper nodded. "Heeya." He dug his heels into his horse's flanks. The laboring mount shot forward, flecks of foam flying from heaving flanks. By now all the horses had dropped away, leaving only the roan racing in front of him. Gradually, he caught up.

"You okay," he called over the wind.

She nodded, her face white against the dark.

His horse faltered, blowing hard. If he didn't want

to kill the horses, they'd have to drop the pace.

"Let's slow it down."

She looked around fearfully.

"The horses can't keep this up."

With a sigh, she reined in. "Where's your friend?"

"There's one more of us. He stopped to pick her up."

"Her?"

"That's right." His voice came out even more rough-edged than usual. He bit back a grimace. His racing blood had kept the grinding ache at bay, but now that the danger had subsided, shards of pain arrowed through his system, his arm throbbing.

"Where could you possibly have left her? There's nowhere to hide around here." Again, she looked around fearfully not noticing his grimace.

"My friend is very resourceful."

"He must be."

His arm hot and warm, he noticed the blood dripping from his fingers plopping and spreading on the dusty ground below.

"Pull up for a moment."

She halted and threw him a questioning look.

He shook his head, wrapped his reins around the pommel and dug a shirt out of his saddlebag, ripped a sleeve off with his teeth and wrapped it awkwardly around his arm.

"You've been shot." Her eyes widened.

"Yeah."

"Shouldn't we get that bullet out?"

"Later tonight will be soon enough. We need to get

as far away from here as we can."

She started to protest, but he held up a hand listening. He drew his gun as he heard the sounds of fast galloping horses.

He relaxed as he saw Sam and Cathleen. His mistake.

Cathleen rode right up to him and fist drawn slugged him hard enough to nearly knock him out of the saddle.

"What are you doing?" The woman riding with them spoke up.

"Who are you?" Cathleen's horse sidled and snorted, reacting to the tension in the air.

"Sherry Lagrange. These men saved my life. And he," she motioned toward Keeper. "Got shot in the process, so keep your hands off him."

Cathleen gave him a cold onceover that sent a chill to his bones, but said nothing. She sharpened like a pointer as her attention moved and stayed on Pardee. "Is he alive?"

"He is."

She reached for her knife.

"Not now." His voice sharp, he straightened. "There'll be time for vengeance later. We've got to get out of here."

She waivered, heat washing through her eyes, her hand hovering on her knife.

Sam rode up and touched her arm, "Come on, Cathleen.

"You, okay?" he asked Keeper.

"I'll live. Let's get moving."

"You think Pardee's friends will be coming after him?" Cathleen asked Sam, ignoring Keeper.

He'd been wrong about her having a steel backbone, Keeper mused. It was made of ice. And why was he getting the cold treatment when Sam was the one that hit her? Maybe they'd made their peace on the trail. Who knew. Women. He'd never understand them.

Sam didn't respond, lifting his horse into a canter.

The rest of them did the same.

"Sam?"

"They aren't coming for Pardee. They're coming for Keeper, Sherry and myself. Dead men—" He glanced at Sherry. "Or women tell no tales. The Caverns has been a well-guarded secret for years. They aren't going to want any of us riding out of here alive."

"I'm Sam Brown." He nodded toward Sherry, galloping beside him.

"I want to thank you, Sam Brown, for getting me out of there. You saved my life."

"I'm happy we could help you."

"Who's your friend?" She nodded in Keeper's direction.

"Keeper Tyree."

"Keeper Tyree?" Her eyes rounded.

"Ma'am." Keeper awkwardly tipped his hat while holding the reins.

"If anyone figures that out, they'll never stop looking for us."

"Well let's hope they don't figure it out then." Keeper spoke through clenched teeth, every jar of his horse's hooves going straight through his bullet-torn arm.

"And you are?" Her voice cooled considerably when she addressed Cathleen.

"Cathleen O'Donnell." She stared back.

Keeper's eyebrows rose. He caught Sam's eye. Sam shrugged. Keeper turned his attention to the horses as Pardee's mount stumbled and bumped into his, causing his horse to sidle into Sam's.

After the horses were back under control, Sam said, "There's a place we can hole up about a mile ahead."

"How can you tell that in the dark?" Keeper shook his head.

"That odd-shaped boulder on the left is a landmark of sorts."

"I can barely see it," Keeper grumbled. "Still and all, you're right. The horses need a breather. No fires though."

"We're going to have to have a fire, you mule-headed gunslinger. Your arm needs seen to," Cathleen ground out.

At least she was speaking to him. That was something, he supposed.

"She's right," Sam spoke up. "If we're behind the rocks, the fire isn't going to be noticeable."

"Fine. Get us there," he pushed out through gritted teeth, his arm aching like a rotten tooth. A muffled sound came from Pardee, trussed over the saddle. Keeper ignored it. He'd keep the man alive long enough to hang but other than that, he wasn't concerned about the sidewinder's comfort. In fact, the more uncomfortable the better. He'd earned it when he murdered Cathleen's son. He might be more than a little irritated that she'd deceived him, but that didn't mean he didn't want justice on her behalf, even if he couldn't trust her.

They rode on. The horses' hooves thumped against the earth, an occasional saddle squeaked as riders shifted tiredly, and boulders threw stark, long shadows across the trail.

The horses dropped to a tired walk. The pain in Keeper's arm ran down to his fingertips and back up his shoulder, like glass pushing through his blood. Finally, Sam threw up his arm and reined in his mount. The pinto tossed his head up and down and snorted. Sam rose in the saddle, looked around then tapped the horse's flanks and disappeared into the rocks on their left.

"He's always doing that," Keeper marveled. "Just disappears into nowhere." He clucked to his mount and headed into the fissure, barely visible in the dark. His horse and Pardee's fit through the narrow opening —just. Pardee's head banged against the side of the rock, his hat long gone. He gave a muffled squawk. Keeper kept riding. The women followed.

Sam had already dismounted and was hobbling his horse as Keeper reined in. Leather creaked as he threw a stiff leg over the saddle and dismounted, biting back a groan. He strode to Pardee's mount, pulled out his knife and slit the ropes holding Pardee in place. The man went tumbling to the ground then rolled out of the way as his mount sidled nervously. With one hand, Keeper pulled him up and tossed him against the boulder. Pardee squawked.

Keeper yanked the kerchief out of his mouth. "You got something to say?"

"I'll kill you for this."

A shadow flitted across the boulder and Pardee's face. Keeper whirled.

Off her horse and racing forward, Cathleen whipped out her knife. As she drew back her arm, Keeper shoved her to the left. Instead of landing in Pardee's black heart, the knife landed in the beefy section of Pardee's forearm.

"You bitch," he howled.

"Now is that anyway to talk to a lady?" Keeper backhanded him then picked up the knife.

"I'm bleeding," Pardee screamed.

"You'll live."

"What did you do that for?" If Cathleen wasn't screaming too, it was the next thing to it. She grabbed for the knife.

He shoved it into his belt.

"Give that to me. It's my right." Her voice rose thin and shrill, her eyes wild.

Sam's gaze flashed back and forth between them, his face impassive. Sherry watched stiff and wide-eyed.

"I can't let you do it. Killing a man stains your soul."

"It's my right I tell you." She beat at his chest, wild with the need for vengeance.

"Cathleen, listen to me." He gave her a little shake with his one good hand. "Listen to me. Have you ever seen a man hang?"

She shook her head.

"It's grizzly. The noose tightens till he can't breathe. He's dangling, with his feet kicking air and his eyes protruding. Pardee doesn't deserve the quick ending you were going to give him."

She threw herself on his chest, sobbing wildly. He gathered her close.

"Cathleen." His voice soft, he buried his face in her hair, then ran his fingers slowly down her arms.

Brittle energy flowed through her to his fingertips.

She drew back and scrubbed her face with her hands. "Don't. I've buried my husband and son and don't wish to bury anyone else that matters. I have no emotion left in me except vengeance and you've robbed me of that."

He dropped his hands and stepped back.

Turning her back on him she disappeared into the trees.

"Stay where I can see you," he called after her.

There was no response.

"I'll go after her," Sherry volunteered then she too was swallowed up by darkness.

"That woman has put up a shield cold as winter between her and everyone else," Sam observed, watching her disappear into the underbrush.

"She has enough passion to light firecrackers if she'd let herself." Keeper's gaze fixed on the dark outline of scrub she'd disappeared into.

"So, what do you intend to do about it?"

Keeper jumped as if stuck by a sharp-pronged stick. "What can I do? She doesn't want me." He had to remind himself he didn't want her either.

Sam shook his head. "There are rare moments I find you keenly knowledgeable. This isn't one of them."

Keeper's jaw dropped.

Sam grabbed the horses and moved to the edge of the clearing and drew off their saddles.

"Hey, is somebody going to see to my arm? I'm bleeding like a stuck pig." Pardee complained, his features pasty.

Keeper ignored him, staring into the underbrush, fingering his vest pocket that held Maybell's ring.

CHAPTER 14

Sam built a fire and saw to the horses.

Keeper leaned against a boulder, the cold soaking into his skin and making him shiver in spite of the fire. He could swear he heard the rush of water over rock.

"Is there a stream nearby?"

"Look across and up."

He did so. Water poured down the side of the mountain. "Well, I'll be damned. Where does it go?"

"It drops to a stream about forty feet below."

"Huh. Give me the coffeepot and canteens and I'll fill them." Keeper pushed away from the rock that held him upright.

"Stay put. You aren't looking so good."

"Maybe you'll bleed to death, old man," Pardee sneered.

"I've got just enough energy to shut you up." He started forward.

A rustling in the underbrush had him whirling gun in hand. Sam straightened, reaching for his.

The two women came tromping out.

"I'll help you." Sherry veered toward Sam. Keeper studied her in the firelight. She appeared to be a few years younger than Cathleen, a head shorter with more meat on her bones and a mane full of chestnut hair. She'd be a pretty little thing when her face healed. His fist clenched, he looked at Pardee. Whose face at the moment didn't look much better. Before he could take a step forward, Cathleen came toward him.

"Give me my knife."

"Ain't happening."

"I need to see to your arm."

He snorted. "More like you want to kill Pardee."

"I never made any bones about that. But what you said makes sense. I'd rather see him hang."

"I don't trust you, Cathleen."

"You can take care of my arm, you pretty little thing." Pardee gave her a lascivious sneer.

Cathleen spat on him then turned back to Keeper. "Sit down and give me the knife."

"Nope."

"You're such a baby."

A strangled snort came from Sam.

Cathleen turned to Sam. "Give me your knife, Sam."

He handed it to her, handle first.

If Keeper's eyes had been bullets, they would have drilled holes in him.

"What?" Sam asked. "I trust her."

Keeper eyed her warily, ready to grab the knife out of her hand.

"Sit." She pointed to the ground.

With a creak of joints and old bones, he did. Figuring he could always tackle her if needs be.

"Hold out your arm." She squatted beside him.

"Oh, for Gad sakes."

She pierced him with a look, her mouth a straight line, waiting.

Resigned, he stuck out his arm.

With a deft movement, she sliced his sleeve from cuff to upper arm then cut it off at the shoulder. The sleeve fell away. Blood dripped steadily on the ground.

"I need to get it cleaned to see how bad it is."

"Can I help, Cathleen?" Sherry hung the old granite pot over the fire then straightened.

"If you could get me a wet rag, I'd appreciate it."

Looked like the women had made peace. Thank goodness. There was nothing worse than two fighting females.

Sherry turned her back and began to rip her petticoat. She trotted to the stream flowing down the mountain, wet the remnant in the rushing water, hurried back and handed it to Cathleen. She looked at Keeper's arm with real distress.

"What can I do?"

"First I've got to see if the bullet's in there." Cathleen pushed a stray strand of hair out of her eyes with a knuckle.

"It is," he said through gritted teeth as she gently washed his arm.

She whitened. "It will have to come out." She handed Sherry the knife. "Heat this in the fire."

Sherry nodded and took it with a shaking hand.

Keeper eyed the knife in the flames and barked, "Sam, got any rotgut?"

Sam didn't respond, just picked up his saddle bag, brought back a bottle, uncapped it and handed it to Keeper who took a huge gulp, his Adam's apple bobbing. Then handed it back.

He looked at the set of Cathleen's jaw and the knife now in her hand and said uneasily. "Wouldn't you rather have Sam do that?"

She bared her teeth in a grimace that was supposed to pass for a smile.

"You left us no choice back there you know." His gaze couldn't seem to leave the purplish hue that marred the perfection of alabaster skin and perfect bone structure.

She didn't answer. Just jerked up his arm.

He grunted.

Even Sam was beginning to look a bit uneasy.

"This is going to hurt you a lot worse than it's going to hurt me."

"Get on with it."

Knife sliced flesh.

He bit down on a scream that tried to fight its way between his chompers. Sherry knelt beside him and took his hand. Beads of sweat broke out on his forehead.

Pardee leered. "How's it feel, old man, to be cut up like a prime piece of beef?"

Sam strode over to Pardee and shoved a bandana in his mouth.

Keeper gave a jerk of approval with his chin in Sam's direction.

Sam nodded.

Keeper bit his lips to keep any sound from escaping as Cathleen probed the raw flesh of his arm. Her face white, beads of sweat on her forehead matched his own. The hand on his hot arm ice-cold.

She looked him in the eye then returned her attention to his arm and dug down.

Hot flashes of fire rolled through him. His nostrils flared and his breathing grew heavy, but he remained still as the boulder he leaned against.

She gave another sharp probe then flipped the bullet out. It rolled onto the ground leaving a bloody trail behind it.

He jerked once then fell back against the rock breathing hard.

Cathleen slumped on the ground and threw the knife away. Her arms on her knees, she dropped her head.

Once he got his breath back, he rasped out, "Thank you."

"You're as tough as a tanned buffalo hide." She shook her head.

"I'm not sure if I've been complimented or insulted."

She didn't respond.

Sam shoved the bottle at her. To everyone's surprise she took a healthy gulp. Her eyes widened and she coughed till her face reddened. When she had herself under control, she poured a healthy amount over his arm.

"That's a waste of bad whiskey." He took it from her and took another healthy swallow.

Sherry nudged her out of the way and began to wrap his wound then made a sling and wound it round his arm and tied it behind his neck.

"Thank you, ma'am."

"No. Mr. Tyree, thank you. You saved my life."

He squirmed, uncomfortable with any type of praise. "Oh, that was mostly Sam."

"It was the both of you. I've told Sam I'm grateful."

"How'd you end up in there?"

"He kidnapped me." She pointed to Pardee, hatred in her eyes.

"Well, we'll get you back to your people." Talking kept his mind off the fire raging in his upper arm.

"I don't have anyone to return to." Her eyes dropped to the ground.

"I'm sorry to hear that." He was gentler with her than he was with most. There was so much loss in her eyes. He didn't know her full story, but he knew it wasn't a happy one.

Cathleen threw him an unreadable look.

"What do you intend to do now?"

"I'm a school teacher. I'll have to find a place to teach where people don't know what happened. And if I can't teach, I'm handy with a needle. I can always set up shop as a seamstress."

"People can be judgmental that's for sure. But those who are, tell 'em to go straight to hell. You've got nothing to apologize for."

For the first time a real smile spread across her features.

"Bet you didn't know Sam's daddy was a school

teacher."

"No, I didn't." Sherry threw Sam a look of surprise. Sam nodded.

"Appears you've got something in common."

"Playing matchmaker, Keeper?" Cathleen asked, studying him with her chin in her hand.

"Wouldn't dream of it. I think the rotgut went straight to your head."

As if she hadn't heard him, she asked, "Do you have an arrangement with your landlady?"

He nearly dropped the bottle he'd brought to his lips. "What makes you think that?"

"I notice you don't deny it."

Sam guffawed. At Keeper's hot look, he turned it into a snort.

"I don't deny. Nor will I answer the question. Frankly, Mrs. O'Donnell, it's none of your business."

CHAPTER 15

Keeper woke with an aching head, fire in his arm and the smell of fresh brewed coffee teasing his senses. The sun hit the horizon and lightened both the sky and the sandstone surrounding them, turning the boulders a pretty pink.

Seeing he was awake, Sherry poured him a cup and brought it to him.

"You're a jewel." He saluted her with the tin cup, wisps of steam rising from the battered mug in the crisp morning air.

She blushed. He noted the bruises were starting to fade. He'd been right. She was a pretty woman. He took a sip of coffee. "Good coffee."

"He says that to all women who serve him coffee."

Cathleen who'd surprisingly slept next to him, sat up, yawned and stretched, pulling loose fabric tight over well-formed breasts. Keeper hastily looked away. "Only if it's true and it's certainly true of this cup of coffee."

"I can't believe Sam hit Cathleen and you let him." Sherry looked shyly at the ground.

Apparently, Cathleen had shared that little piece of information, giving the devil his due, he being the devil. He set down his coffee. Suddenly, it didn't taste so good. "It's nothing I'm proud of."

A rustle of the underbrush had him reaching for his gun.

Sam stepped into the camp.

"It was the only thing we could do to keep her from going into The Caverns."

"Why ever would you want to go there?" Sherry's eyes widened.

"To kill. Him." Her eyes hot as coals, her gaze drilled into Pardee.

"What did he do?"

Looked like Cathleen hadn't told her yet.

"Murdered my kin."

Pardee's eyes widened.

"I'm sorry." Sherry's voice soft, she handed Cathleen a cup of coffee.

"So am I."

"They were right to keep you from going in The Caverns." She shuddered. "I'd never willingly go back."

"Given the right circumstances, you'd do things you would have never considered." Cathleen thumped down her cup and strode into the underbrush.

Sherry started after her.

"Let her be." Sam stopped her with a hand on her arm.

Pardee made muffled sounds through his gag. Keeper pushed to his feet, strode to Pardee and yanked it out of his mouth.

"I need to relieve myself and I'm hungry. You didn't feed me last night."

Keeper grabbed him by the back of the collar and hauled him to his feet. He fumbled in one of his vest pockets and tossed a key to Sam. "Recuff him, with his hands in the front.

"Don't do anything stupid."

As Sam inserted the key, the handcuffs clicked and Pardee dropped his hands to his side, his gaze speculative.

"Don't even think about it." Keeper drew his gun and aimed it at Pardee's head.

Pardee held one hand in front of him and whined. "The other arm's too sore to move."

"I'll be happy to move it for you." Keeper threw him a wolfish smile.

Wincing, Pardee lifted his sore arm then held them both in front of him. Sam clicked the cuffs in place.

"Well, now that wasn't so hard was it?"

As Cathleen walked back into camp, Keeper prodded Pardee with his gun. "Your turn."

She gave the outlaw a hard stare from eyes like chips of ice, her hand trembling on her knife, the conflict to take him in or finish him writ on her face.

Keeper hurried him out of her sight. Pine cones crunched and twigs snapped as they stomped through the underbrush.

"That's far enough."

Pardee looked around. Keeper could almost see him calculating his odds. The hammer on Keeper's six-gun clicked. "I wouldn't."

"It was worth a try."

"If you want to die."

The bushwacker shrugged, took care of business and they headed back.

"I suppose you're going to starve me too."

"Don't rightly matter to me one way or the other."

They tromped back into camp just as Sam passed out hardtack.

"Hey, how 'bout giving me one of those?" Pardee held up his hands.

Sam looked at Keeper. Keeper jerked his chin. Sam tossed a biscuit to their prisoner.

"Over there." Keeper pointed to a grainy, wide-striped, brown-hued boulder.

Pardee sunk to the ground and inhaled his biscuit.

Sam tossed one to Keeper.

Keeper nodded his thanks and gulped his down. "We better get going. I'd like to make the outpost before dark."

"If you think we might be trailed, do you think stopping there is wise?" Cathleen gave him a sharp look.

"We need supplies. I'll get them while you three keep riding."

"How will you find us?" Sam took a gulp of his coffee.

"I'm not in my dotage. I remember how we got there."

Sam didn't look convinced, but wisely said nothing.

Keeper threw the remains of his coffee on the fire where embers hissed and sputtered. "Let's mount up."

Once again, he tossed the key for the handcuffs to Sam then drew his gun. "Cuff his hands behind him."

The moment, Sam got within reach, Pardee lowered his head and charged catching Sam in the gut, bending him over, then took off for the underbrush.

"Damn fool." Keeper raised his gun and aimed. Before he could fire, a knife went whistling past. His heart jumped to his throat. Pardee dead or alive meant no difference to him, but Cathleen having blood on her hands did.

Pardee screamed as the knife landed in his hind end.

Sam went running after him.

"I never took you for a woman with a sense of humor." Keeper chuckled. "I like that in a female."

"If I'd known that, I would have been telling you a joke every hour." Sarcasm dripped from her voice.

Cathleen turned to walk away and he grabbed her arm. She looked at his hand till he dropped it. He put his good hand in his pocket and rocked on his heels. "Why didn't you kill him when you had the chance?"

"I want to see his legs dangling in the air while a rope chokes the life out of him." She looked him in the eye, her voice cold.

"You—" Before Pardee could finish, he screamed as Sam yanked the knife out of Pardee.

Keeper ambled toward them, his hands in his pockets. "Pardee, you yell like a girl and you're a damn slow learner.

"Sam, you think you can get those cuffs changed this time?"

Sam gave him a sour look, unlocked the cuffs, twisted Pardee's arms behind him and clicked the cuffs shut.

"Toss him on his horse and let's get out of here."

"You don't expect me to ride like this."

"For a stone-cold killer, you sure do whine a lot," Keeper remarked.

Sam tossed him up.

"When my friends come for me and they will, I'm going to enjoy killing both you and the Indian slowly and raping the women."

Keeper, who'd just mounted, nudged his horse till it stood next to Pardee's. "Now is that any way to talk about ladies?" Fist clenched, he drew back his good arm and gave Pardee a punch that knocked him out of the saddle.

"Sam, I thought you put this varmint in his saddle."

Grinning from ear to ear, Sam jerked Pardee up by his collar and threw him on the horse again.

"He's on there now."

Pardee, slumped over the saddle horn, began to groan.

"So he is." Keeper grabbed the reins of Pardee's mount. "Let's get a move on."

The sun rose, changing the sky from dusky grey to a clear blue. White clouds floated lazily above them. The scenic view deceptive as a woman. Keeper had learned death and destruction always waited on the horizon.

The horses, now rested, trotted along the canyon

floor, the rising sandstone walls letting them ride two and three abreast. Sam in the lead, Keeper—with Pardee—bringing up the rear, and the women sandwiched safely between. Though, anyone could get picked off from the top of the canyon, Keeper thought, his gaze constantly moving.

Cathleen moved up by Sam and Sherry fell back to ride beside him. "Do you really think they'll come after us?"

"They'll figure their lives will depend on it and they won't be far wrong."

"You'd ride back into The Caverns after having seen it close up and personal?" She shuddered.

"Wouldn't be my first choice, but if the man I was hunting was in there, yes."

"Hey, my butt hurts," Pardee interrupted.

"You're damn lucky she didn't kill you."

"Who is she anyhow? She's sure got a hate on for me."

"You killed her son."

Pardee shrugged. "Who?"

"Last name would be O'Donnell."

"Means nothing to me."

"A kid in Dodge City."

"Oh him. He should have never been mixing with the menfolk." He gave an ugly laugh.

"Why don't you ride on ahead." He nodded to Sherry. His voice pleasant enough that it would have had people who knew him hightailing it.

He drew Pardee's horse up close to his own. "I talked her out of killing you, but I could fix it where we don't ever have to listen to you again. So, I suggest you be careful what you say. If you know anything about me besides the speed of my gun, you should know I'm a man of my word and I'm telling you here and now, you say one more word to give those women grief, I'll cut that tongue right out of your mouth." He held Pardee's gaze with a cold stare. "You understand?"

Crimson flooded Pardee's rough features then washed to white.

"I said, do you understand?"

Pardee nodded.

"Say it out loud."

"I understand."

"Good." Keeper turned his attention back to the trail.

They rode at a steady pace all day, climbing up rocky paths that wound through the gray and brown rock formations then leveled out with evergreen and ashy-colored, brittle underbrush. An occasional lizard sunned itself on the rocks and small rodents scurried under bushes at their approach. They reached the edge of the arroyo that housed Obadiah's rundown general store and bar near sunset.

Sam reined in and dropped to the ground, his ear pressed against bare earth then pushed to his feet. "Riders coming."

"Behind or in front?" Keeper stood in his stirrups, his restless gaze scanning the horizon.

"Behind."

"Well, we need those supplies." He settled back in the saddle, his arm aching like the very devil.

"What do you want to do?" Cathleen nudged her horse toward Keeper's.

"I'm going to ride on down and get them from that cantankerous ole coot. The rest of you keep heading home. I'll catch up."

"I don't like the idea of separating." Sherry worried her bottom lip with her teeth.

"Me either. But it seems the safest." He twisted toward Sam. "How many riders?"

"Two maybe three."

"Well let's hope they follow me."

"You've only got one good arm," Cathleen pointed out.

"That's all I'll need." It was no braggadocio as he saw it. Just fact.

"At least let me see to your wound before you go." Worry had lightened the icy gray-blue of her eyes and added a touch of warmth. He held her gaze, repeatedly reminding himself she hadn't been honest with him and couldn't be trusted.

"Tonight."

"How will you find us?" Cathleen's horse sidled and she quieted it.

"I'll find you." He tipped his head, since he couldn't his hat, touched heels to his bay's flanks and went galloping into the outlaws' trading post. Dust spurting under huge hooves. A tumbleweed went bouncing by as he reined in his horse. The saddle creaked as he threw a stiff leg over the horse's rump and put a boot on the ground. He watered his horse at a half-filled trough then tied the reins to a nearby post and strode through the dirty doors of the saloon.

He took one look back from where he'd come—the others were gone—and strode into the dimly lit saloon.

"Well, looky here," Obadiah croaked, a grin showing a gold front tooth. "Did you find Pardee?"

"I found him," Keeper responded in his gruff voice.

A handful of men sat playing cards in a corner.

Most of them looked up, curious.

Three rose and sidled through the door.

Obadiah slammed a beer down in front of him. Lukewarm liquid splashed on Keeper's hand.

The wiry old man looked over his shoulder. "Don't see him. Did you kill 'em?"

"Does it matter?" Keeper took a long pull of his beer. It might taste bitter but it went down easy.

"Not to me. So, where's my cleaning crew? You didn't get 'em shot up did ya?" He leaned elbows, encased in a grubby shirt, on the bar that had already accumulated dust. Glass rings standing out against the fine, dirty powder.

"They're safe enough."

"Good to hear. So, you stopped in for a beer?"

"That and some supplies."

"What can you trade me for 'em?"

"Well, I'm not planning on putting on an apron and cleaning your damn buildings if that's what you're thinking."

Obadiah gave out a croaking laugh and slapped a skinny leg in delight.

"Now that's something I'd love to see."

"Ain't happening." Keeper took another deep gulp of his beer, finishing off the contents before he slammed it down on the counter.

Chairs scraped at the card table.

"Well, I guess I'll just have to take your money then. If you live that long." He jerked a pointed chin in the direction of the table and backed up.

Hand on his gun, Keeper turned around.

The three men were spreading out.

Two more appeared at the door to the saloon. Obadiah reached under the bar and pulled out a shotgun and aimed it at the two in the doorway. "Now gents. Let's keep the odds even. You just get along about your business."

They hesitated.

He cocked it. "Now."

They melted away.

"You call three to one good odds?"

"Well, yeah. If you didn't have that injured wing, I'd have let 'em in. Now get it done." And with a suddenness that took Keeper by surprise he dropped to the ground.

"Let's see what you got, ole man," the one on the left called out. He wore a poncho, chewed on a cigar and was at least ten years younger than Keeper. He flexed his gun hand, a confident smile on his pockmarked face.

Keeper put his hand to the bar and eyed the other two. They appeared even younger, but still seasoned. One on the stocky side. One tall and thin. They wore ponchos too. The one on his right moved restlessly causing his spurs to jingle.

"Today's your day to die, ole man." The one in the middle bared his teeth in a smirk. His eyes glistening with the eagerness of a predator ready to make his kill. The one on the right wore a similar expression.

"I'm getting real tired of being called old." And like lightning, his gun was out. He crouched firing left to right.

The men fell like dominoes, stunned surprise on their faces. The man on the right had drawn his gun. As he crumpled, his finger tightened on the trigger. The smell of sulfur filled the saloon.

"Tarnation." Obadiah's knees creaked as he rose from behind the bar, rubbing the side of his head. "Any closer and that bullet would have taken half my ear. You owe a couple of double eagles over and above whatever your supplies cost for the mess."

"You're a crook, you know that? I'll haul their carcasses out into the street."

"They'll leave a trail of blood that will stain the floors."

"You've got to be kidding me. There's enough old blood stains on your floor, you'll never need to paint it."

Obadiah cackled again.

Keeper grabbed the closest by a boot heel and drug him across the floor, leaving the trail of blood the saloon keeper had predicted.

"Be careful. When you get to the door, there'll be two more waiting for you."

Keeper jerked his chin in acknowledgment. When

he got to the door, he hauled the lifeless man to his feet and pushed him out in front of him.

Shots rang out. Keeper bulled through the door, dropped the man, whirled and fired at the hombre on his left then his right. The two men crumpled to the ground. He backed cautiously into the saloon and waited. Nothing moved on the streets.

"I may have to charge you another double eagle, to make up for all my clients you're killing off." The old man cackled.

"Yeah," Keeper said dryly.   "Let's get those supplies."

Half an hour later he swung into the saddle as the sun flirted with the horizon, haloing the sandstone badlands in shades of pink and red, softening the hard rocks with its palette of color.

He studied his surroundings, his horse's shoes ringing against rock as they trotted through buttes and occasional brown prairie grass. As he neared a narrow path through the canyon a rider blocked it, rifle drawn.

"You're blocking my way, mister." Keeper wrapped his reins around his saddle pommel, brought his horse to a stiff-legged halt, his hand on his gun.

"You came to the Caverns uninvited."

"You got a problem with that?"

"Me and every other resident that uses it."

"And you came by yourself to deliver this message?"

"My friend went after the rest of your party. As soon as I take care of you, I'll be joining up with him."

"Then I suggest you get to it."

"You in a hurry to die?"

"Not hardly." In one smooth motion, Keeper's gun was in his hand. He ducked and fired.

The stranger pulled the trigger as he toppled from the saddle. The sidewinder's shot went wide, hitting sandstone. Rock sprayed and caught Keeper's horse on the shoulder. Screaming, the bay sidled. Keeper settled him down then leaped out of the saddle. He toed the hombre, who lay face down, over. He didn't recognize him.

The man looked up at him his breathing labored. "Who the hell are you?"

"Keeper Tyree."

"Keeper Tyree. Well damn me." He closed his eyes and died.

Keeper bent down, rifled through his vest and came away with three double eagles. At least it would put a dent in the money Obadiah had lifted from him. The men he'd killed had been carrying little to no coin. He climbed back in the saddle and without a backward glance rode away.

As the sun went down, stars came out. With the velvety darkening of the sky came a huge bright moon that lit the deep canyon floor, occasionally throwing long shadows from the tall rocks across his path. He rode steadily for a couple of hours, hoping he didn't ride right past one of Sam's hidey-holes.

Someone stepped out of the shadows. With his good hand, he pushed the reins into his hand cradled against his chest by a sling and whipped out his gun.

"We expected you an hour ago."

"Sam." Relieved, he holstered his gun. "That's a good way to get yourself shot."

"I'm not sure there's any good way to get shot."

"Yeah." Keeper swung off his horse. "Did you have any trouble?"

"Someone was following us, but he rode on by about an hour ago."

"He'll be waiting for us up the line. Have you found a place for us to bed down?" Reins in hand, Keeper walked beside Sam, leading his horse.

"Up ahead." Sam pointed. They wound around large boulders and came into a clearing, hidden from the trail, where a fire crackled and orange flames danced merrily. The scent of strong coffee teased his senses. Pardee was sitting on the ground, leaned up against a boulder with a rag stuffed in his mouth. He balanced on one flank, the cheek he'd been knifed in hoisted in the air.

Sam followed his gaze. "I didn't want him yelling out to whoever was back there."

"Have you seen to him?"

"Yup, he's all tucked in and ready for bed."

Pardee stared at him, hatred in his eyes.

Cathleen saw him and pushed up from the rough-barked log she'd been sitting on. Her gaze swept over him. Her shoulders visibly loosened. She poured a cup of coffee and brought it to him.

"Thank you."

Sherry grabbed jerky and hardtack and held them out. Sam took his horse.

"That's not necessary," he protested, as he sat down the coffee and took the food.

"Sit and eat," Sam said.

Used to riding alone, the companionship and kindness warmed him. He sank down on the opposite end of the log Cathleen had vacated, wolfed down the biscuits and jerky, and swallowed down his coffee.

Cathleen, who'd disappeared into the shadows, came back carrying a canteen and rags. She stopped in front of Keeper. "Take off your shirt."

"I beg your pardon." His eyebrows rose.

"You heard me. No point in ruining another shirt."

"My shoulder's fine."

Blue eyes bore into him.

"Fine." He fumbled with his sling, wishing his body wasn't quite so old and beat up. Thank goodness, his muscle hadn't run to flab, but his chest and arms had enough scars and holes to scare a body away.

She undid his sling then reached for the tails of his shirt and tugged. He took a step away. "I can manage. I ain't crippled."

Tapping her toe, her arms crossed, she waited.

Awkwardly, he slid out of his vest then yanked the shirt over his head. He came out of it to see Sherry and Sam watching him. Sam winked then strolled toward him and held out a flask.

"Thanks." He took a healthy swig and then handed it back.

"Sit." Cathleen pointed to the log behind him.

"Who wore the pants in your marriage anyway?" he muttered as he sank down on the rough bark, pine needles crunching as he shifted his heel.

Cathleen ignored the question. Instead, she gave a swift jerk and yanked off the bandage, coated with crusted blood.

A grunt escaped him.

She gave him a quick look then started to clean the wound. "I don't see any infection." Relief came through in her voice and she dabbed at the hole in his shoulder. As she rewrapped it, firelight played across her face and his chest and torso making a long scar gleam. She tied off the bandage and then ran a light finger down the scar making his skin jump and quiver. "Where did you get this?"

"Bringing in Jesse Barr."

"This one?" She touched a short deep scar.

"Tiny Graham," he said through gritted teeth and straightened. "Thankee."

"Put your shirt on and I'll re-tie your sling." She handed him his shirt.

He dove into it and as soon as she retied the sling, shot off the log. "Is there a stream around here?"

She gave him a bewildered look.

Sam grinned and pointed behind him.

"Don't say a word," Keeper growled as he strode past him. A branch snapped under foot as he tromped to the stream. Ignoring his throbbing shoulder, he squatted in front of a warbling brook, the moon glistening bold and bright in the stream. He splashed water on his face over and over with his good hand. By the time he'd finished his dampened shirt clung to his chest cooling down his overheated system to the point he shivered.

For the life of him, he couldn't figure out what about the widow he found so attractive. He liked a good armful in his bed. Shake the sheets and you'd never find her. She was stubborn as a mule and just as contrary. And most of the time she eyed him with disdain. No, not exactly disdain, but disapproval, with a rare lightning flash of warmth. And yet, in odd infrequent moments, he saw banked passion and promise. And it drew him. More than it should.

He shook his head. There was no fighting nature. The heart had a mind of its own. He snorted. Thank goodness he didn't have one. With that bracing thought he stomped back into camp.

Everyone had bedded down, except for Sam who stood with his rifle cradled in his arm. He nodded when he saw Keeper. "Get some sleep. I'll take first watch."

Keeper put a finger on his forehead then pointed it at Sam. "Wake me and I'll take the next watch."

"I will."

"I want to head out at daybreak." He strode to his saddle and blanket that someone had laid out for him, crawled into it and pulled his hat down over his eyes.

He'd barely closed his eyes when someone shook his shoulder. He fisted his good hand and struck out.

Sam ducked and chuckled. "Your watch."

"Everything okay?" He sat up and scrubbed his face.

"Yes. I made some fresh coffee."

"I appreciate that. Get some shut-eye, I'll wake you

at dawn."

Keeper pushed to his feet, stretched, snatched his rifle, leaned it up against a cedar tree near the opening of the clearing then grabbed a cup of coffee.

"Good coffee, Sam," he said in a low voice and could have sworn he heard Cathleen snort.

He grinned and shook his head then turned up his collar and burrowed into his duster. The night air chilly enough to raise goosebumps. Still and all it was a beautiful night. A thousand diamond-bright stars and a big full moon with a tinge of yellow to its shine broke the deep indigo night.

Almost of its own accord, his gaze fell on Cathleen, the blanket drawn up to her ears and her hat pulled down to her nose. He would have loved to have known her before. Before the death of her son had turned her features brittle and her eyes to ice. He hadn't missed the times her gaze fell on Pardee, darkening with hate, while her hand hovered above her knife.

Ah well. Life was never easy and seldom as we wanted it. He leaned back against a nearby oak, his knee bent, his heel on the rough bark of the tree and sipped his coffee, waiting for dawn.

It blew in on a chill, light breeze, snuffing out the starlight and bringing a pink hue, as pretty as a woman's blush, to the sky. He shook Sam's shoulder. "It's daybreak. You take care of Pardee. I'll see to the horses."

Sam came awake with disconcerting alertness. He pushed to his feet and headed for the underbrush. "You get the horses and I get the mule."

"Yeah." His lips quirked up.

"Ladies." He woke the women.

Sam came tromping back and led Pardee into the underbrush and when they came back, fed him. Since the man had a knife slash in one arm and could barely raise it, and a knife hole in his butt, they'd left the cuffs in the front instead of drawing his arms behind him.

They ate quickly and mounted their horses as the sun broke over the horizon, leaving everything in its path golden, and warming Keeper's stiff neck. Their mounts plodded steadily up a path that got steeper and more dangerous. Sam leading, the women in the middle then Pardee who kept lifting up his sore fanny and Keeper bringing up the rear, loose rope knotted on Pardee's saddle and the end of it on his.

By evening they would be out of the badlands. Keeper just hoped they could get through it without breaking their necks. Yards up ahead, they'd be traveling single file, leading the horses, boulders on one side, a straight drop to certain death on the other.

His gut tightened and the air grew close.

"Sam," Keeper called.

Sam dropped back beside him.

"Somebody's back there."

"Did you see anybody?" Sam shot him a look, then turned his attention back to guiding his horse along the canyon floor.

"No, it's more a feeling." Keeper rubbed the back of his neck, where the hair on it stood on end.

"What do you want to do? Once we start on that

narrow piece of trail there'll be no going back."

"Get the women and the horses across. Pardee and I will bring up the rear. Hopefully, if there's any shooting, Pardee will catch the hot lead."

"That's the way you want to play it?"

"That's the way."

Sam nodded and trotted his horse back to the front of the line and stopped when they reached the narrow trail. Sam swung out of the saddle. Keeper followed suit. White-faced, Cathleen did the same.

"Why is everyone dismounting?" Sherry asked, her expression anxious.

"It's too narrow to ride across. Too dangerous."

"I can't. I'm afraid of heights." Sherry looked over the edge and swayed in the saddle.

"You've got to do this." Fighting back his impatience, Keeper glanced over his shoulder.

Nothing moved on the horizon.

"I can't. You'll have to go without me."

"Well, I can't do that." Keeper turned his full attention on her. Here was a problem he hadn't been expecting.

"Sherry." Sam held out his arms and she reluctantly dismounted. He took her hand and spoke gently. "I'll be right there with you. I'll send my horse across. He's taken the path so many times he can do it in his sleep. Just you and me. Okay?"

She bit trembling lips, her nerves palpable. The tension stretched. Finally, she nodded.

"Good girl." He squeezed her hand then turned to his horse. He tied the reins around its neck and started it forward. The pinto began to clomp across.

Sam turned and gave Sherry an encouraging smile. "You're next."

She gave him a frightened look. "I thought you were going next."

"I'm going to bring your horse." Holding her mount's reins, he took her fingers in his other hand. "You can do this."

Biting her lips, she took a firmer grip of his hand and started across, hugging the wall with her free hand.

"Don't look down," Sam cautioned.

She nodded and edged on, one foot at a time.

A pebble bounced down the canyon wall. She stopped and swayed.

"I've got you." Sam's voice lyrical and soothing.

She started forward again. Inch by inch she crept along the narrow trail. As they neared the other side where the lip widened, Keeper asked, "Are you ready, Cathleen, or would you rather Sam come back and take your horse across?"

"I can get myself and my horse across." She lifted her chin.

"Then get'er done."

She started across, talking quietly to her mare. About the time they reached the center of the trail, Sherry crossed over onto the wider portion of the trail where the danger of falling dropped off drastically. As soon as Sam and her horse joined her, she turned and hugged Sam. "Thank you. I couldn't have done it without you."

"You would have managed."

"No, no I wouldn't." She gave him one last squeeze and let him go.

"Well, Pardee, looks like it's your turn." This is where it got tricky. Getting Pardee across and hoping whoever was out there didn't kill his horse or shoot him in the back. He waited then heaved a sigh of relief as Cathleen stepped onto firmer, wider ground.

Pardee looked at the narrow passage with rock on one side and nothing but air on the other. "Not happening."

Keeper yanked him out of the saddle.

"Now what?" Pardee sneered.

"Keeper," Sam called. "Hold on, I'll come and get his horse."

"Appreciate that, Sam."

"Now we wait."

Sam crossed as lithely as a mountain goat. He took the reins of Pardee's mount. "I'll be back to get your horse."

"You heard the man," Keeper told Pardee.

"Doesn't mean I'll cross."

"Oh, I think you will." Keeper yanked off his sling then pulled his gun.

Sam got Pardee's horse across then came back for Keeper's bay. As soon as he was on the narrow ledge and headed across, Keeper nudged Pardee in the ribs. "Let's go."

"At least take the cuffs off."

"It's not happening. Now get moving."

Reluctantly, Pardee started across, Keeper on his

heels.

A shot rang out. Rock splintered at Keeper's shoulder. Up ahead the horse neighed and sidled. One hoof went over the ledge. The animal screamed in fright. Sam got him under control and kept going, reaching the other side.

Keeper twisted in the direction of the shot and saw the gunman on the ledge they'd come from, gun in hand, ready to shoot again. Keeper drew and fired in one swift motion. The man toppled from his horse.

Pardee saw his chance and lunged at Keeper. Keeper slammed his head with his pistol and knocked Pardee backward. Pardee flailed and fell over the side, into wide open air, grabbing Keeper's leg as he went over the ledge.

"Keeper," Cathleen screamed.

Pardee's weight pulled Keeper over the side. He grabbed the edge as he fell, hanging on by his fingertips. His bad shoulder screaming.

"If I go, you go," Pardee yelled, hanging on for dear life.

Keeper felt his fingertips slipping. He couldn't bear Pardee's weight and his own, especially with his bad arm. Blood spurted and ran down his back where muscle strained.

His fingers slipped further.

Time to make his peace with the Almighty.

As his fingers slipped again, a knife went zitting through the air. Pardee slumped and his hands fell away. Then he went plunging to the rocky ground far below.

"Give me your hand, Keeper." Cathleen reached for him. Sam right behind.

"Get back, Cathleen. I'm not going to have you go tumbling after Pardee."

"Move back now, Cathleen, and let him climb up." Sam touched her arm.

"Alright, but if you fall, I'll kill you."

He grinned in spite of himself and started to pull himself up, inch by painful inch. Looking for toeholds with his boots. Pebbles rattled death cries as they went tumbling down the arroyo, making the hair on his arms stand up. He crawled up another inch, then another. Finally, he lay face down on the narrow trail, panting. After a couple of deep breaths, he lifted his head. "It may not be dignified, but I'm thinking of crawling the rest of the way."

"That's fine by me. Let's just get off this ledge." Cathleen's heart thudded so hard he could hear it.

Sam steadied Cathleen as she pushed cautiously to her feet. Carefully they crept to the ledge on the other side.

Keeper pulled himself to his feet and cautiously followed. Arms reached for him and yanked him forward.

Sam and Sherry hugged Cathleen. Then Sam pounded him on the back. Sherry shyly hugged him.

"That was close," Sam said.

"Yeah."

Cathleen walked a short distance away and stood with her back to them, her head bowed, her shoulders shaking.

He strode to her. "Cathleen."

"I thought I'd lost you." She threw herself into his arms, clutching him.

Surprise jacked through his system. For a long moment he stood motionless then drew her close.

"Thanks to you, I'll live another day."

She just clutched harder.

"Pardee is out of your life for good."

She dropped her hands, sniffed and wiped her eyes. "So he is." A note of surprise to her voice. "My son can be at peace now."

"Can you?"

"We'll see."

"Let's get you home."

They mounted and rode. The trail out of the badlands wider and easier going.

Tyree pulled alongside Sam. "Where will you be going now?"

"Don't rightly know." Sam shrugged.

"If you're looking for work, I know someone who's hiring."

"Yeah?"

"I'm sure Maybell in El Dorado could use a good man. Just tell her I sent you."

"I'll look her up. Thanks."

Keeper twisted in his saddle. "Where are you going, Miss Sherry?"

Surprisingly color flushed her pretty features. Before she could respond. Sam said, "She's coming with me."

Keeper gave a start of surprise. Cathleen blinked.

And Sherry gave a smile that lit up her face.

"We talked about it last night. If I can teach fine. If not, I'll set up as a seamstress. El Dorado works for me."

"I think it's a mighty fine idea," Keeper said.

"So do I." Cathleen nodded emphatically.

"We'll ride with you to Dodge then cut over to El Dorado."

"Well now that's settled let's pick up speed and get on out of here."

Four days later they pulled into Dodge City, stopping in front of the sheriff's office.

"Thank you." Cathleen held out her hand to Keeper. He took it, always surprised at how small it was in his large paw. When he didn't let go, she tugged. He dropped it.

She gathered up her reins. "I better be getting home."

"I'll see you home, Cathleen."

"That won't be necessary," she said quickly.

He started to object. Sam looked from one to the other and spoke up. "We can see her to her place then head out from there."

"Will you be able to collect the bounty on Pardee?" Cathleen asked.

"Yeah, the sheriff knows me. If it's any problem, I'll have him talk to you. It really should go to you anyway. You killed him."

"You getting it was the original agreement, remember?"

"I remember. Are you alright?" He gave her a

searching look, unable to get a good read on her. She'd been self-contained and distant since she killed Pardee. He hoped with time, she'd heal.

"I will be. I'll be seeing you."

She gathered her reins and nudged her mount forward with Sam and Sherry following.

"I doubt that," he said under his breath.

He watched them ride away until they were out of sight. "Well, that's that," he said to no one in particular.

CHAPTER 16

Keeper sat at his table at Molly's, rattling the paper, occasionally reaching for his coffee. It had been over three weeks since they'd returned to town.

"Ready for your breakfast, hon?" His landlady came back and refilled his mug.

"No."

"I'm worried about you, Keeper. You ain't eating and I'm betting you aren't sleeping either. You've dropped ten stone. If I'm ever in your bed again, I'll probably lose you if I shake the sheets."

His face warmed and he rattled his paper louder. He'd given Molly one excuse after another for not bedding her when he got back. Truth was she just didn't appeal anymore. Nor could he work up any interest in any of the other ladies that would be only too happy to accommodate him and take his coin. "I'm fine, Molly."

"Well, I'd say we are about to be finding out." With a thump of the coffeepot onto her tray she hustled away.

He had no idea what she meant by that. Didn't much care.

A lady's fancy hat with a turquoise ostrich feather

in it landed on the table, crumpling his paper.

He looked up and blinked. "Cathleen? Mrs. O'Donnell?"

He sprang to his feet. He'd only seen her in black or men's pants. Not decked out in turquoise and pink paisley taffeta that fit her body in all the right places and looked like glory.

He gulped, his throat dry and finally managed to push out, "You're looking mighty fine."

"Thank you."

"Where do you keep your knife in that getup?"

Holding his eye, she stuck her leg on a chair and raised her skirt till it hit her thigh. Riding a shapely white leg like a garter rode a knife holster.

"Oh, I see." He continued to stare, fascinated. Couldn't look away, in fact.

The material rustled as she dropped her dress. "Aren't you going to ask me to sit down?"

He pulled out her chair and waved her in with his arm, then scooted up her chair when she sat down. He dropped into his own hard wooden seat. "Want some coffee?"

"No thank you."

"What brings you here?" Whatever it was, he was damn glad to see her. The whole damn room had brightened since she'd walked through those doors.

"I've got a job that needs doing and no one else is capable of taking it on, seeing it through."

"Well." He looked down at his coffee cup and moved it around on the table. Finally, he looked up. "You need somebody else killed?" Surely, the little girl hadn't been hurt. A hot band squeezed his forehead till she made a dismissing motion.

"No, nothing like that. This is more of a permanent commitment." She looked him right in the eye.

He'd felt like his skin didn't fit for weeks. Now suddenly, everything fell into place. "Why, Mrs. O'Donnell, are you asking me to marry you?"

"And if I were?" Her color heightened but she held his gaze, her eyes a warmer shade of blue than usual, more violet, downright beckoning in fact.

"I'd have to say no."

"Well then, I guess there's nothing more to say." The face so warm and open before became shuttered. She pushed upright. Her body once more reminiscent of the brittleness in it when he first met her.

He stood too.

When she started to walk away, he grabbed her arm and yanked her against him. "I like to do my own proposing."

"Then I suggest you get to it." Her voice crisp, her eyes dancing again.

"Mrs. O'Donnell, Cathleen, would—"

"Are congratulations in order?"

Molly stood with the coffeepot in her hand. Her eyebrows arched. Sadness lurked behind her jaunty expression. It gave Keeper a start. He'd always thought she was just out for some fun too. He should have known better.

"He hasn't asked me yet." The words came out through a tight smile as the women eyed each other.

Keeper shifted on his feet. "Molly, I—"

She made a dismissive gesture with her hand. "I told you she was trouble when she came through that door. What I didn't add was for me." She straightened her shoulders and walked away as another couple entered the dining room. Molly shooed them off. "Kitchen's closed folks." Then disappeared herself.

Cathleen raised an eyebrow and gave him a knowing look.

He ran a finger around his collar that suddenly felt too tight. He cleared his throat. "I need to tell you I've taken another job." He'd dropped his arms and they stood staring at each other.

"Oh?"

"You're looking at the new sheriff of El Dorado."

"And you were just going to leave, ride away without saying good-bye?"

"Cathleen, I've got a heart as black as sin and a soul just as bad. I knew you could do a whole lot better. But if you're willing to overlook it, I certainly am. Would you accompany me to El Dorado as my wife?"

To his surprise, she looked stricken. "I can't."

His heart stumbled. "You can't?"

"I can't leave Henry."

Then it righted again. "Bring him along."

She hesitated.

Nerves skittered up and down his spine and he thrummed his fingers on his thighs, his palms damp.

Silence stretched as she stared at him unblinking. Finally, a smile twitched at the corners of her mouth, lifted her cheeks and lit her eyes. "In that case, I'd be honored. And that black heart of yours is mainly exaggeration and wishful thinking."

"I've never had anybody tell me that before." He hauled her into his arms and kissed her as he'd longed to since the first moment he'd seen her striding into the dining room, the sun haloing her, turning that magnificent mane of hair to ebony.

She returned his kiss with fervor and a promise of tomorrows and new beginnings.

CHAPTER 17

Two Months Later in El Dorado

An organ hit the first notes of a wedding march from the front of the little white church that sat at the edge of town. The music drifted on the air competing with horses' hooves, shouting and an occasional gun blast. Still the rowdiness, and deadliness, had dropped considerable since Sheriff Tyree had been sworn in.

He stood now in the front of the church, sweating bullets, his tie choking him, his gaze fixed expectantly on the house of worship's foyer, Sam at his side. Maybell stepped into view in a blue silk that showed off her full figure. She held a posy of blue and purple wildflowers and a smile as wide as the Kansas sky.

With a whisper of silk, she stopped across from him and gave him a wink. Some of the nerves jumping between his shoulder blades loosened.

Aislinn and Jacob came next. Aislinn strewing blue flowers over the gleaming mahogany aisle. Jacob, looking as uncomfortable in a new suit as Keeper felt, carefully held a frilly white pillow. Maybell's ring balanced at its center.

The twitch between his shoulder blades took another notch down. He was going to be a pa. He already loved the little minx as much as her momma. Catching his eye, she ran the rest of the way down the aisle and gave him a huge hug. His heart swelled and he drew her into his arms, bussed her soundly then let her go.

Jacob continued his cautious approach, his eyes never leaving the ring.

The music swelled.

As if drawn by a magnet, his gaze arrowed to the entryway. Cathleen stood with her arm hooked around Henry's. The sun caught the colored glass and haloed her like an angel. His poor ole heart hitched then began to pound hard in time with her steps down the aisle, the cream-colored silk she wore rustling with each step. Over the past few months, she'd gained a little weight. She'd never be an armful like Maybell or Molly, but she filled his arms just fine. Her eyes had lost the ice in them and were now, more often than not, filled with warmth and laughter. Today they were his favorite shade of violet. Her gaze, behind the veil, caught his and held. She gave him a heavy-lidded look that had him positively blushing.

Henry halted before the altar and placed her hand in Keeper's. "You take good care of her and treat her right or you'll answer to me." His eyes suspiciously bright.

"You have my word."

Henry nodded then took his seat next to Ezekiel who tried his best to plaster a smile on his face. Juanita sat next to him and whispered something in his ear that had him giving a brief smile and nod.

The minister stepped forward dressed in his Sunday best-black and holding his bible. An earnest young man with spectacles that kept slipping down his nose.

Cathleen turned to Keeper and he took her hand. Warmth and electricity shot through him as he stared at their entwined fingers. Her hand delicate in his large, callused paw. This moment the most sacred of his entire checkered life.

She smiled at him and he smiled back, trying to telegraph the love he felt for her. Words had never come easy. He only hoped she knew what was in his black heart.

The minister cleared his throat.

"We are here today..." The words washed over him, his whole being concentrated on Cathleen, till he heard the minister ask, "Do you take this man to honor, love and obey?"

"Of course, but I expect him to do the same."

Laughter rippled through the audience. Maybell actually guffawed. "She's a keeper, Keeper," she shouted out, which brought on more laughter.

"You got that right, Maybell," he called back not taking his gaze off his bride.

The preacher turned to Keeper and made the same request.

"I do," Keeper answered.

"Then by the power vested in me, I now pronounce you man and wife. You may kiss the bride." He beamed at them.

Keeper yanked her into his arms and did so with

enthusiasm. And Lordy, Lordy, she was kissing him back just as eagerly. Finally, he drew back, his pulse jumping all over the place. "Mrs. Tyree." He grinned.

"Mr. Tyree."

He squeezed her hand.

They turned to face their guests. As his thigh brushed against hers, he started as he felt the hard edge of her knife holstered on her thigh. His eyebrows rose to his hairline. He leaned down and whispered to her, "You're wearing your knife to your wedding?"

"Somebody has to have your back, Sheriff."

"I gotta say I've never had a prettier guard, Mrs. Tyree.

"I don't think I'll ever get tired of saying that." He just couldn't seem to stop grinning.

"And I'll never get tired of hearing it."

Maybell's bellow interrupted as she hustled down the aisle. "Come on you two. We're having a reception at the Pink Monstrosity and the entire town is coming."

He looked down and for the first time noticed their guests had departed. Even Sam and the kids had disappeared. "Shall we?" He offered her his arm and she took it. They meandered down the aisle, gazing into each other's eyes and grinning like loons. Who'd a thought an ole coot like himself would end up acting like a teenager, but there it was.

They strolled through the door and were pelted by rice. He threw up an arm to protect them as they hurried down the steps, laughing. An aisle of people stretched from the church to the Pink Monstrosity.

Looked like the whole goldurn town had turned out. Good thing Maybell had elected to hold it on the rental side of the monstrosity where Ezekiel was housed and the town café. Several of the God-fearing women of El Dorado were in the wall-to-wall aisle.

He propelled them along as pellets of rice dropped down his collar. Finally, they reached the wide white veranda and hustled inside. The kids stood waiting, Aislinn jumping up and down.

"Are you really, my poppa now?"

"You bet. And this seals the deal." He stooped down, gently took her hand and slipped a ring on it, as close to her momma's as he'd been able to find.

She held up her hand and admired it. "Thank you so much. What does it mean?"

"It means we're a family."

She gave him a gap-toothed smile that warmed his heart.

"Now that's settled let's go get cake." She took Jacob's hand and went racing off.

Cathleen turned to him her eyes a deeper violet, than he'd ever seen, luminous and glistening. And something more lurking in them that he couldn't quite read.

She laid her hands on his chest. "You're right, Sheriff Tyree."

"Hmm, about what?" Distracted by his reaction to her hands on him.

"That sealed the deal." And kissed him soundly.

AUTHOR'S NOTE

A few factoids.

There was a Long Branch Saloon in Dodge and it's still around. The materials for building it were provided by soldiers when they lost a ballgame.

Anheuser-Busch was the first beer served at the Long Branch.

Between hay and grass means half-grown.

Bug juice is booze.

Prostitutes were called calico queens and or soiled doves.

And you may already know that zitting around then was used as we use zipping around or flying around now.

The information gleaned from one of my favorite sites: https://www.legendsofamerica.com

If you would like notification of upcoming releases, just drop me a note and mention new releases in my contact form at: http://www.sandracoxwriter.com.

Last but not least, if you enjoyed *Keeper Tyree* enough to leave a review, thank you so much. A good review or rating is an author's bread, butter and favorite ice cream, all rolled up in one. I can guarantee you'll put a smile on my face when I see it.

I leave you with a wish for many exciting reading-adventures and a thank you for taking time to read my story.

S.